AMARYLLIS NIGHT AND DAY

AMARYLLIS

NIGHT AND DAY

RUSSELL HOBAN

BLOOMSBURY

Lines from 'Life is Just a Bowl of Cherries' Words and Music by
Lew Brown and Ray Henderson © 1931 DeSylva, Brown & Henderson, Inc.
Lyric reproduced by kind permission of Redwood Music Ltd (Carlin),
London NW1 8BD
Lines from 'Walking Spanish' by Tom Waits reproduced by kind permission
of Warner Chappell Music Ltd.

First published 2001

Bloomsbury Publishing Plc, 38 Soho Square,
London WIV 5DF

A CIP catalogue record for this
book is available from the British Library

ISBN 07475 5285 1

10 9 8 7 6 5 4 3 2 1

Typeset by Palimpsest Book Production Limited,
Polmont, Stirlingshire
Printed by Clays Ltd, St Ives plc

ACKNOWLEDGEMENTS

The author acknowledges the following: *Mazes and Labyrinths*, W.H. Matthews (Longmans, Green & Co, 1922); *A Walk on the Wild Side*, Nelson Algren (Rebel Inc., an imprint of Canongate Books Ltd); *Aphorisms*, Georg Christoph Lichtenberg (Penguin, 1990); and *Notes from a Friend*, Anthony Robbins (Fireside, 1995).

My thanks to:

Adam Lawson, my driver and companion on research trips to East Sussex and Oxfordshire; Graham Collins, Proprietor of the Birling Gap Hotel, East Sussex, for weather information for 31 December 1993 and 1 January 1994; the owners of Troy Farm, Oxfordshire, for permission to view their maze; and Roger Lade of the Little Angel Theatre, for showing me the *Sleeping Beauty* marionettes backstage.

I am very grateful to Martha Fleming who, in June 1999, guided me through her exhibition, *Atomism and Animism*, at the Science Museum, and put me in touch with Alan Bennett, the Klein-bottle artist. I am deeply indebted to Alan not only for the time and the information he gave me but also for his generosity in allowing me to involve him in a fictional dialogue with Peter Diggs.

Hearty thanks to Robert Ellis, whose remarks in our Klein-bottle discussions helped me to focus my own ideas and get this novel started.

My special thanks to Dominic Power, who read many drafts and revisions and gave me encouragement and useful comments; here I must also thank our friends at Il Fornello in Southampton Row for years of amiable forbearance while manuscripts were read over very long lunches. They are, in order of appearance, Manolo; Bruno; Juliano; Paco; Jesús; Carlos; Rino; Mario; Jesús Díaz; María; Luigi; and (appearing nightly) Aldo.

R.H.
London, 22 February 2000

To Liz Calder

'Once I, Chuang Chou, dreamed that I was a butterfly and was happy as a butterfly . . . I did not know that I was Chou. Suddenly I awoke, and there I was, visibly Chou. I do not know whether it was Chou dreaming that he was a butterfly or a butterfly dreaming that it was Chou.'

'Chuang-tzu', *Encyclopaedia*
Britannica Online

'There is a balm in Gilead
To make the wounded whole;
There is a balm in Gilead
To heal a sin-sick soul.'

Afro-American spiritual

'Never play cards with a man called Doc. Never eat at a place called Mom's. Never sleep with a woman whose troubles are worse than your own.'

Nelson Algren,
A Walk on the Wild Side

CONTENTS

1

THE FIRST TIME

The first time I saw her was in a dream, the colours were intense; the air was full of vibrations; everything seemed magnified and slowed down.

The street lamps were lit but the sky was still light. She was waiting at a bus stop. A sign said BALSAMIC although there was nothing vinegary about the place, no friars and no Gilead in sight. There were nondescript buildings in warm colours, perhaps leaning a bit, perhaps painted on canvas. She was waiting for the bus; there were obscure figures queuing behind her.

At first she had her back to me, then she turned as I drew near. She had long straw-coloured hair, blue eyes. She was very thin and very pale; her face was fine-drawn and haggard. She was wearing a white T-shirt with music staves and notes on the front of it, faded jeans, white plimsolls. She looked at me and clenched her fist like a tennis player who's just scored a difficult point at Wimbledon. 'Yes!' she shaped with her mouth, didn't say it out loud.

A bus was coming. No number on it, only the destination: FINSEY-OBAY. Not a place I'd heard of. The bus was a tall and delicate thing of bamboo and rice paper, sheets of yellow, orange, and pink pasted together and candlelit from within like a Japanese lantern. It was much bigger than a doubledecker, towering so high above me that even when I tilted my head back I couldn't see the top of it.

Still with her eyes on me, she beckoned to me to follow as she boarded the bus. A thrill of terror ran up through me from my feet; I stepped back and woke up, cursing my cowardice. I tried to get back into the dream but I couldn't, and I was left with a sense of loss that stayed with me. I searched in my *A to Z* for anything Balsamic but there was nothing.

2

EMPTY SPACES

'A sense of loss pervades the paintings of Peter Diggs,' wrote the critic Cecil Berkeley about my last show at the Fanshawe Gallery. 'His palette is muted, his compositions unsettling. The figures in his pictures seem about to depart, and there are odd empty spaces that make the viewer wonder who or what has gone and who or what is coming.'

But that's life, isn't it? And those of us who think about the empty spaces tend to paint pictures, write books, or compose music. There are many talented people who never will become painters, writers, or composers; the talent is in them but not the empty spaces where art happens.

3

THE SECOND TIME

The dream stayed with me so strongly that I could play it back like a videotape: the bus stop in the summer dusk, the street lamps lit against a sky still light – that time of day that always catches at my heart.

There was the sign that said BALSAMIC; the letters were sharp and clear; they riffled like rail departures but the name stayed the same. There were those shaky-looking buildings and the bus stop and there she waited, the thin woman with the straw-coloured hair, blue eyes, and pale face, unknown but seeming to look at me round the edges of my memory. Sleeping or waking, I'd never seen her before.

Again and again she gestured with her clenched fist and said, 'Yes!' silently. She wanted me to follow her. Why? Here came the bus: FINSEY-OBAY, yellow, pink, and orange rice paper and bamboo lit from within like a Japanese lantern. Such a light against that not-yet-dark sky! Again she looked at me as she boarded the bus and I felt that thrill of terror as I stepped back. And again the sense of loss. What did she want? How could I find her again?

She was gone; I was left behind in the present moment which is not a simple finite thing measured by the clock; it's a palimpsest of all the present moments before it, their images, music, words and whispers rising up through the layered years from the oldest present moment to the newest; and in those moments live, remembered or forgotten, sleeps and wakings and dreams.

I'm what is called a figurative painter; that is to say, I can draw, and I paint recognisable things: people; monsters; midnights; manhole covers; pillar boxes, whatever. The only world we know is the picture-show the cerebral cortex puts together from sensory data. Whether there's anything else nobody can say. Vermeer listened to the ticking of the world and painted a series of magically arrested moments that argue reality. Still, if reality had a stage door I'd hang around there to see what comes out after the show.

As preoccupied as I was with the dream woman, my commitments in the waking world still required my attention. I teach *Images and Ideas* at the Royal College of Art on Tuesdays and Thursdays. Tomorrow was a working day and I needed some new material. Sometimes unknown images offer hints of themselves; glimmers of things half-seen, almost remembered, come into my mind so that I go looking for them without being certain of what I'm after. I hadn't been to the Science Museum for a long time so I thought I might have a wander round there later. Mrs Quinn comes in to clean on Monday afternoons so it's a good time to be out of the house.

In the morning I put in some time on a painting I'd begun a couple of weeks ago, *The Beckoning Fair One*, a title borrowed from an Oliver Onions story. The cloaked woman in the painting appeared seven times: as the foreground figure she was facing front; receding from the viewer she turned in overlapping successive images until she was seen from the back at the edge of a cliff overlooking the sea, her fair hair streaming in the wind. Whenever I looked at that painting there ran through me the thrill of terror I had felt in the dream, as if I too were at the edge of that cliff, about to step off. The images in my pictures tend to be uncomfortable ones. I tend to be uncomfortable myself.

Her face was ghostly and unfinished but I was surprised by how much she reminded me of the woman in the dream. I always tone my canvases before I start, using a thin turpentine wash of colour. Expecting things to go fairly cool, I'd done a warm undertone to work against, a mixture of cadmium yellow deep and cadmium orange. As the picture developed, however, I found it moving away from cool, so that I was letting the undertone show through and harmonising warms with warms. I like it when a painting begins to find out who it is and starts to go its own way. In the cool and exacting north light from the windows and skylight the picture was becoming its present moment.

After lunch, with my head still feeling a little strange from last night's dream and the morning's work, I went to Fulham Broadway tube station. The aeroplane-hangar effect of that place holds daylight and darkness in different ways at different times and varies its voices and silences and echoes similarly, although the rails always cry, *Wheats-yew! Wheats-yew!* as the trains approach. Today the hangar seemed full of waiting, holding its breath to see what would happen next. Beyond the hangar arch the great brass gates of the sunlight stood open. People on the eastbound platform leaned against pillars, sat on benches or stood singly and in groups. They read books and newspapers. They ate and drank and threw rubbish on the floor. They spoke into telephones or murmured to one another. They looked across the tracks to the westbound platform where other people leaned, sat, stood, read, ate, drank, threw rubbish, spoke, murmured, and looked back at them. Pigeons plodded here and there. *We too*, they mumbled.

Wheats-yew! Wheats-yew! cried the rails. The tunnel opened its mouth, lights appeared. Bigger, bigger, bigger grew the train. TOWER HILL, shouted the front of it. *You!* hissed the train. It opened its doors and swallowed me up with other eastbound souls. Inside the carriages the eastbound faces hid whoever was behind them. The train rattled and rumbled, it shook and swayed out of daylight into darkness muttering warnings and prophecies and crooning to itself like an old mother or an ancient sea. In the darkness the present lost its hold and the past, stirring in its sleep, turned its face to me and whispered a name.

4

NAMELESS HERE

'Lenore,' I said on a long-ago day, 'how does it feel to walk around in a name out of Edgar Allan Poe?'

'Nameless here for evermore,' she said. 'Names are pretty useless, really. If you say the name of anything ten or twenty times it scatters and falls away and the thing that's named stands there all naked and unknowable. Sometimes it comes to me that nothing can be known, nothing at all. Black is the colour, silence is the music, Spanish is the way to walk.' She liked to be baffling, or at least gnostic, whenever possible. Whether she actually walked Spanish I couldn't say, but her walk was well worth seeing from the rear.

'Your main attraction,' she said to me, 'is that you're going to make me unhappy.'

'Why is that an attraction?' I said.

'We haven't made love yet, but when we do I know that each time I feel you in me I'll feel the time when you leave me. It's something to look forward to.'

'Is it something you *want* to look forward to?'

'Yes. Life is mainly a series of disappointments. People tell lies and for ever usually lasts only a month or so and nothing turns out as promised. So when I can depend on a thing ending as I expect it to that's a thrill for me, it's a solid satisfaction, it's a treat.'

'You must be a very unhappy person, Lenore.'

'Well, I've tried being happy and it doesn't work. Don't you want to kiss me and make me feel better?'

5

NEW AND STRANGE

At South Kensington I rose from the depths, escalated to the upper world, passed through the arcade and the queue at the 14 bus stop, crossed between the cars and walked up Exhibition Road where soft ice-cream and hot dogs sweltered and coachloads of emptiness waited for their children to return. The sunlight, crazed with detail, explored every wrinkle, whisker, pore and pimple of tourists consuming Coca-Cola, mineral water, coffee, tea, hot dogs, soft ice-cream, exhaust fumes, and culture.

The sunlight explored me as well as my footsteps joined those of generations of children, mums, dads, teachers and others all the way back to the heavy tread of Roman legions marching with their standards and centurions up Exhibition Road to the Victoria and Albert, the Natural History, and the Science Museum thirsting for dinosaurs, volcanoes, Indian bronzes, William Morris, and steam locomotives. Not only was I prepared to have empty spaces in me filled with wonders, I was vaguely excited and expectant, as if the sluggish air were alive with possibilities.

Bannered and mighty with knowledge, the Science Museum loomed. Grateful for the relief, I stepped into the coolness.

In the museum shop a young male sales assistant stood among marvels and schoolgirls and again and again threw a tiny aeroplane that returned to his hand every time. Through the turnstiles I passed and found my way to Martha Fleming's installation, *Atomism and Animism*. Borrowing from various of the museum's collections she had arranged objects in new and provocative combinations supported by her texts.

Guided by a brochure I passed from one part of the exhibition to another, I shook my head over the model of a slave ship placed next to one of the *Mayflower*; I had long thoughts about Lapointe's pastel box, each stick of colour labelled with a word perhaps from dreams; I pondered deeply the metaphysical implications of Joshua Reynolds's *camera obscura*; I was entranced by the motionless galloping horses on the disc of Muybridge's zoopraxinoscope, imagining the disc at midnight beginning to move, then spinning faster and faster as the many horses of stillness became one midnight galloper circling with its speechless rider through the hours of darkness.

There was a beautiful sixteen-inch ivory model of a nude woman, supine, lying as if exhausted by love. Her body was open; some of her organs remained inside the cavity and some lay near her. There was something more than medical about the model, as if a team of little ivory anatomists and philosophers had determined to solve the mystery of the female once and for all; they opened her up, they reached into her and took out various parts, they said, 'Aha!' and 'Oho!' and nodded their heads but the mystery remained. It was evident that this had been understood by the carver. Might it have been a woman? I imagined a smile on her face as she worked.

I was from time to time overwhelmed by waves of schoolchildren and tour groups; overlappings of voices, echoes, and echoing silences moved with me as I progressed from floor to floor into and out of centuries, cultures, and continents until eventually I found myself, silent among the voices and footsteps, standing in front of a display case full of Klein bottles in a variety of shapes, a glittering array of ins and outs beyond my comprehension. As I stood there I had a sensation of wearisome reiteration and the idea of something continually passing through itself.

This feeling came of course from the Klein bottles, which I'd looked up at various times on the Internet. *Encyclopaedia Britannica* defines a Klein bottle thus:

> *Topological space, named for the German mathematician Felix Klein, obtained by identifying two ends of a cylindrical surface in the direction opposite that necessary to obtain a torus. The surface is not constructible in three-dimensional Euclidean space but has interesting properties, such as being one-sided, like the Möbius strip (q.v.); being closed, yet having no 'inside' like a torus or a sphere, and resulting in two Möbius strips if properly cut in two.*

I didn't understand that definition myself. Klein bottles were a mystery to me and I like mysteries, but this one seemed to have a metaphor lurking in it and I didn't like that. If those bottles had something to tell me, let them come right out with it, was how I felt about it.

There are lots of websites on the Internet devoted to Klein-bottling, with all kinds of graphics and animations. Here's an illustration from one of them:

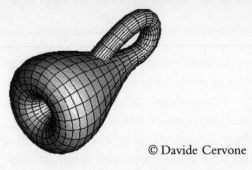

© Davide Cervone

'The Klein bottle cannot be *embedded* in three-space, but it can be *immersed* there,' it says at that site. I love that. Another site says, 'Any Klein bottle in three-dimensional space must pass through itself somewhere.' Great.

The fact that a Klein bottle 'is not constructible in three-dimensional Euclidean space' hasn't stopped people from having a go at it. The many variations on the Klein-bottle theme in the case had been made by a glass-blower named Alan Bennett. I tried to imagine him getting his mouth around those involutions and I couldn't. I started to read the card in the display:

Series of Glass Klein Bottles by Alan Bennett

These Klein bottles were made for the Museum by Alan Bennett during 1996. Bennett was interested in the relation between the Klein bottle and the Möbius strip, a one-sided surface featured in case N17. He tried to construct Klein bottles which could be cut to form Möbius strips with more than one twist. He found that simply coiling the inlet tube produced Möbius strips with the corresponding number of twists when the bottle was cut, and that he could cut Klein bottles along certain lines to produce Möbius strips with large numbers of twists. Surprisingly, he found he could produce a single Möbius strip from a Klein bottle.

Following this were descriptions of these twenty-nine bottles that were shamelessly flaunting their metaphysical intestines for anyone who cared to look. I needed not to see them for a bit so I turned my back but I felt their presence like a box of live cobras behind me.

When I turned again I saw my reflection, as before, in the glass of the case and fragmentarily repeated in the Klein bottles. Then another face appeared beside mine. I spun around and there she was, dressed the same as in the dream, watching me thoughtfully. She was better-looking than I remembered and not really all that thin. Her dream self might have been painted by Edvard Munch on one of his less cheerful days but the real woman was quite different. Her hair was darker than in the dream; she was still pale but her paleness was that of those Pre-Raphaelite nymphs done by John William Waterhouse; like them she had an exquisite figure, delicately chiselled features, big innocent eyes, and a look of sadness and regret, as if she knew she'd be big trouble but was sorry about it. Astonishing, really, how she was so recognisably herself and yet so unlike her dream self.

She was carrying a heavy shoulder bag which thumped to the floor when she unslung it. 'Well,' she said, 'here we are.'

'You!' I said. 'I saw you in a dream!'

'And I saw you, but why didn't you get on the bus?'

'I don't know,' I lied. 'I just hesitated and then I woke up.'

'You're lying,' she said without any emphasis, her voice as clear and sweet and refined as a character in a BBC Jane Austen. 'What were you afraid of?'

'You're very direct, aren't you.'

'You're American. I thought Americans liked directness.'

'I wasn't afraid of anything.'

'Lying again. Was there something about me that put you off?'

'Jesus,' I said, 'you don't let go of a thing, do you.'

'I don't pick up anything I want to let go of. *Was* there something about me that put you off?'

'Not at all!' I said. I couldn't tell her to go away and stop bothering me, she was too beautiful. 'I've told you, I didn't get on the bus because I woke up.'

'All right, whatever you say.' She looked at me the way a betting man might look at a horse. 'But I need you to stay with me longer than that, I need you not to wake up too soon.'

'"Not to wake up too soon!" I don't think I've been asked that before. You need me to stay with you in a dream? I don't understand that. And I don't understand how you managed to get into my dream when I've never seen you before in my waking life.'

'It wasn't your dream, it was mine. I brought you into it because I tuned in to you. I wasn't sure I'd connected, though, until you turned up at the Balsamic.'

'You call it "the Balsamic" as if it's a place you're very familiar with.'

'Too true.'

'You often wait there for the bus to Finsey-Obay?'

She folded her arms across her chest and hunched her shoulders as if she were cold. 'More often than I'd like,' she said, looking past me.

'So you pulled me into your dream because you wanted company? You were lonesome? What?'

'I didn't want to ride that bus alone.'

'Why not?'

'I'd ridden it alone before and I didn't like it.'

15

'Why didn't you like it?'

Still looking past me, she said, 'That's enough for now, OK? Answering all these questions is like taking my clothes off in a cold room.'

'OK, but would you tell me how you tuned in to me, how you connected?'

'Do you spend a lot of time looking for what isn't there?'

'I spend a lot of time looking for what *is* there – that's what I do.'

'In what way?'

'I'm a painter, but what's that got to do with tuning-in?'

She closed her eyes and hugged herself. 'I spend a lot of time looking for what isn't there.'

'While looking away from what *is* there?'

She half-turned away from me. The curve of her cheek was like a little plea for mercy. 'How I tuned in to you: in my dreams I'd been waiting three nights for this bus that I didn't want to take and I wasn't looking forward to another night of it. Then yesterday afternoon I was at South Ken tube station and I saw you on the westbound District Line platform. You were reading H. P. Lovecraft, same edition I've got, so I thought you might be worth a try and I tuned in to you. Did you feel something happening?'

I tried to remember. I get a lot of strange feelings, strange thoughts. Maybe there'd been a moment as I stood there when I was suddenly full of sadness. But then I often have those moments. 'I'm not sure,' I said. 'How did you tune in?'

'I just sort of aimed my thoughts at you.'

'You just aimed your thoughts at me and connected and then you pulled me into your dream. Not a lot of people can do that.'

'It hasn't done me much good so far.'

'You do this sort of thing often?'

'Why, do I look like a tart?'

'Don't be so quick to take offence – if I say the wrong things it's because this is all so new and strange to me.'

'New and strange can be a lot better than old and familiar.'

I made a little noise with my mouth and shook my head to convey that you never know. 'You said that in your dreams you'd been waiting for that bus for three nights and you didn't even want to get on it. So why go on waiting? Was anybody forcing you to?'

She didn't stamp her foot but she looked impatient. 'The dream always starts at the bus stop. Do you remember the neighbourhood it was in? There's no place I wanted to walk to from there, it's all too nothing.' She shuddered. 'And you can't get a taxi around there and there never are any cars along that road to give you a lift.'

'Is there perhaps more to it than that?'

Her face closed up a bit. 'How much do you need to know?'

'More than you're telling me.'

'I'd rather not say everything out, all right?'

'I don't need to know everything but I need to know more about you and that bus.'

She looked at me as if she didn't like me very much. 'Right: me and that bus. Once the dream starts and I'm at the bus stop I'm stuck with it; if the bus comes I have to get on, I haven't got a choice. I don't want to get on the bus but I have to. That's how that dream works. Are you satisfied now?'

'There's no need to get angry with me – you want me to

17

ride that bus with you and you can't blame me for being curious about the whole thing.'

'Jesus, am I that hard to be with? Have I lost my looks all of a sudden?'

'You're beautiful and probably you're charming when you're in the right mood and I'm delighted to be your companion but why did you pick me? You must have family or friends who could help you with this.'

'No family and no friends I'd want to bring into that dream.'

'But you brought me into it.'

'Look, if this is all too much for you just say so and I'll find somebody else.'

'No, no, it isn't too much for me – it's just that I feel a little crazed. Please don't be offended but you're not a vampire or anything like that, are you?'

'Do I look like a vampire?'

'You look like a Pre-Raphaelite nymph but that doesn't rule out the other.'

'Well, I'm not going to suck your blood, if that's what you're worried about.' She turned her back on the display case. 'I don't like Klein bottles,' she said. 'They make me feel like what's the use.'

'But you came to the place where the Klein bottles are. Did you know you'd find me here?'

'It seemed a possibility. And now I'm going.' She slung her bag.

'Want to go for a coffee?'

'Good idea.' She flickered a smile at me.

I picked up her shoulder bag, she took my arm as if we were a couple. Amazing. We were out of the museum by then, going down Exhibition Road. She had a Pre-Raphaelite

18

walk, as if she wore mythical garments that didn't cover too much. I hadn't had a woman to walk with for a long time; her breast was touching my arm and I wouldn't have minded walking right through the afternoon to the twilight and the Balsamic bus stop with her. When she wasn't talking she seemed very vulnerable. Sometimes as she turned to look at something I'd see the curve of her cheek and I wanted so much to protect her that I was all choked up with it. Protect her from what? Lenore's face came to me and I looked away. I wondered what this one did for a living.

'I teach piano,' she said without being asked.

'Is that Chopin on your T-shirt?'

'Mazurka No. 45 in A Minor.'

'That's my favourite one.'

'Really?'

'Really.'

'Do you play?'

'No, I just listen to it on CD.'

'Whose recording?'

'Idil Biret – she gets the dance in it and the shadows.'

'Hum it.' She covered the staves on the T-shirt with her hand.

'You needn't do that – I can't read music.'

'Hum. Or whistle if you'd rather.'

I whistled it as far as I could and when I stopped she said, 'Flat,' but nodded and indicated with her face that I had passed the test. 'I have that recording,' she said as if she had just heard it. 'Why is No. 45 your favourite?'

'It's like the ghost of itself, as if it's in the past and the present at the same time.'

'Balsam through itself.'

'What did you say?'

'Passing.'

'Through itself?'

'Mm.'

Coaches and tourists, soft ice-cream and hot dogs approached and receded. It was a grey and sweating sort of afternoon but with her beside me the light and air were different, as if this footage had been shot by the same cameraman who did the dream. Near the tube station we stopped at the Greenfields Café, subtitled Sandwich Emporium, which offered tables on the pavement under an awning. She saved our table while I went inside and got the coffee, then we sat there looking at each other while the world and his wife and children walked past with cameras, maps, bottles of mineral water, and loud voices in several languages. A man in shorts and a string vest passed us, singing, 'I love you, I love you,' into his little telephone.

'I'm Peter Diggs,' I said, extending my hand.

'My name's Amaryllis.' She tilted her head a little to one side to watch my reaction while she shook my hand in an absent-minded way.

'To sport with Amaryllis in the shade . . .' I thought, but decided not to quote Milton at her. 'You look like an Amaryllis,' I said. 'It's not a name every woman could wear.'

She nodded as if I'd passed another test. I felt as if I were auditioning for a part; I had to remind myself that she was the one who'd approached me.

'Surname?' I said.

Her hand jumped up from the table as if it were about to take flight, then settled down again. 'Not yet,' she said, brushing away invisible crumbs. 'Do you believe in ghosts?'

'Not the kind the paranormal people are always trying to photograph.'

'What kind then?'

'The ones that live in the mind – no one else can see them – doing what they did and saying what they said in the past, over and over.'

'Why?'

'Maybe because they didn't get it right the first time.'

'Is there a lot that you didn't get right the first time?'

'Yes. What about you? Do you believe in ghosts?'

'I'd rather not but they seem to believe in me.' She said this looking away from me as she did much of the time in our conversation. 'Let's talk about something else now.'

'OK. Has it ever struck you that people are mostly composed of the past? Every new moment immediately becomes the past, and the next moment, which is the future, does the same thing. There's not much *now* to be had.'

'Hmm,' she said, and shook her head, whether sympathetically or not I couldn't tell.

'Where did the Finsey-Obay bus take you last night?' I asked her.

'I don't know; I just kept climbing the stairs until I woke up.'

'Were you afraid?'

'I had to pee. I'd better go now.'

'Why?'

'I need to think about this. I always leap before I look and then I'm sorry later.' She was half out of her chair.

'Are you sorry now?'

'Not yet.' She was walking away. 'Don't follow me.'

'I don't know your last name, I don't know where you

live and I haven't got your phone number. How am I going to get in touch with you?'

'At the Balsamic?' she said over her shoulder as she dwindled towards the tube.

6

THE BRASS HOTEL

'At the Balsamic?' she'd said. Was she going to pull me into her dream again or was she testing me to see if I could dream *her*? Yes! I could feel it in my guts: it *was* a test. She needed me to dream her because she wanted to work something from my end instead of hers. What? Evidently what she wanted from me had more to do with the dreamworld than the one we lived in and worked in by day. Otherwise it would have been too simple, I supposed. Was I being used? I didn't care.

Amaryllis in the flesh had been quite different from the dream Amaryllis. *Her* dream, that had been; so that was how she dreamed herself – thin and pale with straw-coloured hair, almost a ghost of the real Amaryllis who had walked beside me down Exhibition Road. I saw again the curve of her cheek as she turned her face away from me. How many times had I said to my students that the idea was immanent in the image!

Tomorrow was a working day and I ought to have been getting my thoughts together for it but all I could think of was Amaryllis. I didn't want to ride that Japanese-lantern bus but I didn't know how else to see her again, so I poured myself a large whisky and put Takemitsu's *Eclipse* for shakuhachi and biwa in the CD player. The music was spooky and shadowy but it seemed heavy and earthbound compared to those luminous paper yellows, pinks, and oranges; that bus had its route in a dimension I couldn't reach while awake but the more I recalled the Balsamic bus stop the more it began to seem as real and permanent as any other bus stop – it just happened to be in a world I could only get to in a dream. I flung my arms apart as if to open the curtains between me and it but everything stayed the same.

The hours between then and bedtime were perfectly useless as far as work was concerned. I drank, I ordered in a pizza, I watched *The Double Life of Veronique* on video. Then I began to worry that Amaryllis might die in the dreamworld or get stuck there. Finally, at two o'clock in the morning, I dragged myself soddenly off to bed. 'Balsamic,' I said, got my head down, and lay awake until some time between four and five. Then I dreamt I was in a lift in the Brass Hotel. The building was brass and so was the lift and everything else. The other people in the lift looked ordinary enough. We were going up so I waited until everyone else got off, then I pressed the button for the lobby. I went to the brass reception desk where a brassy-looking woman gave me a brazen look and said, 'What?'

'Any brass for me?'

'Who from?'

'Whom. Amaryllis. She looks like a Waterhouse nymph.'

'For you?' She covered her mouth and began to laugh and I woke up.

'What's so funny?' I said. But the Brass Hotel was gone and the receptionist with it. So I'd have to try again. I felt a surge of panic at the thought of not seeing Amaryllis in a dream, not seeing her ever again anywhere. Don't think that way, I told myself. Who knows? Maybe the Brass Hotel is on the Finsey-Obay bus route.

7

VENICE?

The next day was Tuesday, a teaching day. I'd been trying to get my students to loosen up their heads a little. 'Bring me something you've never visualised before,' I'd told them. Some pictured childhood memories, mostly bad ones; some brought in monsters derivative of Bosch and Giger; one heavily Christian young woman did a crucifixion. In the main the images, with the exception of those few that were straight erotica, were unpleasant but not surprising; the mind has its cupboards and its hidden predictables. I tried to find interesting things to say but my thoughts were elsewhere and my remarks bored me even more than the drawings and paintings I was seeing.

The last work I looked at was by one of my mature students, a brooding sort of man in his forties who was a film editor. He was dark, with dark hair and pale-blue eyes. He reeked of cigarette smoke and always needed a shave. His name was Ron Hastings and he'd done a large pastel of a horned Satan wearing pyjamas with a design of yellow, orange, and pink oblong shapes. This Satan had a crocodilian sort of tail and looked as if he might well have fathered Rosemary's baby.

'Interesting pyjamas,' I said.

'He came to me in a dream,' said Hastings. 'The pyjamas seemed to be lit from within.'

'Did he say anything?'

'No, he just laughed and I woke up.'

'Probably just as well you did.' I suddenly had the feeling you get when you reach for something on the top shelf of a cupboard and everything falls on your head. I crawled out from under the fallout and worked up some comments on dream imagery and the exploration of the subconscious. Some discussion developed from this and I encouraged the students to keep pen and paper by their beds so they could catch dreams before they faded. Only one or two seemed more than minimally interested; they all had projects that didn't leave them much time for side trips.

So I got through the day and I went home with Ron Hastings and his Satan in my head. Why can't life be simple? I wondered. But in my experience – I was thirty-four years old – it never had been and I didn't expect it ever would be. What was it with these yellow, orange, and pink luminosities? Dream leakage or what? Might Hastings have been at the Balsamic bus stop at one time or another? Was he an old boyfriend of Amaryllis's? I pictured the two of them together and wished I hadn't. Then I remembered a film called *Dreamscape* in which Dennis Quaid had the ability to get into other people's dreams and take an active part. Quaid was the hero of the film but there was a bad guy who had the same ability and they had to fight it out. Was Hastings going to be my bad guy? In any case, his yellow, orange, and pink Satan was an intrusion that I resented. Could it have been coincidence? I doubted it.

I drank some whisky, ordered in Chinese takeaway,

watched *The Vanishing*, read a bit of *Death at La Fenice*, went to bed, stayed awake, fell asleep, and dreamt that I was in Venice. The sky was leaden, the smell was bad, the Piazza San Marco was choked with tourists and pigeons. I doubted that the Finsey-Obay bus went to Venice but even so I was hoping to find Amaryllis. I looked for her in all the cafés, on every bridge and in every passing gondola and vaporetto but there was no sign of her so I decided to enquire at the Questura.

Asking directions in phrase-book Italian and mostly not understanding the answers I threaded my way *destra* and *sinistra* through little dark streets and over many bridges. The odours were dark and melancholy, they hinted at things better left unhinted at. The smell of the chalk and blackboards of my childhood came to me. Once during the summer holiday some friends and I broke into the school: so many echoes! Such lonesome sunlight. Was I being followed? I kept looking behind me but I was never sure whether I saw or imagined someone dodging out of sight around corners and into doorways. 'I don't need this!' I said. 'Life is hard enough.' Contemptuously, the bronze Moors struck the hour but I didn't know which one it was.

Eventually I found the Questura and was shown into Commissario Brunetti's office. 'Please forgive me for taking up your time,' I said. 'I know you're a busy man.'

'This is your gleam,' he said in perfect English. 'How can I help you?'

'Did you say "gleam"?'

'How can I help you?' he repeated.

'I think someone might be following me.' I described Hastings. 'I was wondering if he might have come to your attention.'

'It this man local or a foreigner?'

'He's British.'

'A tourist?'

'He'd be here like me – visiting.'

'Has he threatened you, this man? Menaced you in any way?'

'No, not really. It's just that I've got a bad feeling about him.'

'Ah! A bad feeling! At this moment there are more than a million tourists in Venice and most of them give me a bad feeling. But even in my own gleams I haven't the resources to do anything about it unless they actually commit a crime. I'd be happy to balsam if I could but . . .' He shrugged and spread his hands with the palms upturned and I woke up.

'Wait!' I said. 'I forgot to ask you about the woman who looks like a Waterhouse nymph! Her name is Amaryllis, she has blue eyes!' Too late.

Two dreams without Amaryllis. Could do better.

8

OLD WOMAN AS BLACK CAT

My third attempt gave me a feeling of desolation and an old woman posing as a black cat. I'd dreamt her many times before; she looked like the old witch in the Grimm story who sent the soldier down into the hollow tree for the tinder-box. She was never very convincing as a black cat but she enjoyed the pose and she liked to speak in what she fancied was a feline manner. Her cat costume was nothing more than a shabby black poncho and a black sombrero but she believed in it. She was sitting on the steps of a little shack somewhere on a lonesome road with pine woods on both sides.

'How long has it been?' she said purringly. 'Souven years?'

'You mean seven?'

'I speak as I find,' she said. 'Have you been practising unnaturally?'

'I'm looking for Amaryllis. Have you seen her?'

'Do you pine for her?'

'Yes.'

'Bawl some?'

'It might come to that.'

'I have where to lay your head, you know.'

'Not yet,' I said.

'Please yourself. But keep in mind there is a bomb in Gilead.'

'You mean balm?'

She spat, opened the door of her shack, and went inside as I woke up.

9

EVERYBODY HAS ONE

In 1993 when I started teaching at the Royal College of Art Lenore was in her last year there. I'd taken over from Julian Webb who'd died suddenly, and on my first day I was looking at portfolios and putting faces to the names on my list. I had twelve postgraduate students, most of them in their twenties: seven women and five men. Their work was of a high standard – untalented people don't turn up there – with the usual variation in originality and interest. Despite our being in what has been called 'a post-skill era' in the visual arts, all of them could draw, which cheered me immensely. It won't stop global warming or make the air fitter to breathe but it makes me feel good.

As far as I know, plain girls are not rejected by the RCA – it just happens that female art students in their twenties tend to be a good-looking lot, and my seven were all eye-gladdeners. Being a man I couldn't help noticing this, and being visual-minded I was pleased by it.

Lenore could have done well as an actor, I think. Her face was striking, she had long black hair with a fringe; she had commanding black eyebrows; she was wearing black jeans that she could only have zipped up while lying down, a black leotard, and black motorcycle boots. She was able, without appearing to make an effort, to be more *there* than the people around her so that I found myself watching her as I made my way from student to student and portfolio to portfolio.

When I got to Lenore I asked her what she was working on and she said, 'Seeing.'

'What have you seen lately?' I said.

Stacked up on one side of her carrel were four hardcover notebooks. She handed me the top one. It was yellow and had the number 21 on the cover. I opened it and found notes and sketches on every page. The handwriting was small and elegant, almost calligraphy. 'Have a look at yesterday's page,' she said. I turned to it and read:

Twenty-seven people in this carriage and each one has a different death inside. These deaths are like animals.

Following this were sketches of people sitting side by side, Underground passengers evidently. They were very good drawings; her eye was sharp and her hand was sure. Another note below the sketches:

This one's death is a little dog that barks all the time; that one's is a crocodile that waits with only its eyes sticking out of the water. Someone else's is a brown rat that scurries and sniffs with its nose twitching. Everybody has one, and all of them are different.

She was looking up at me in a challenging way. 'What's yours?' she said.

She caught me off balance with that one. 'My death?' I said. 'You tell me.'

'An owl, I think, waiting to swoop down on the mouse of you.'

'You see me as a mouse?'

'How do *you* see yourself?'

'Mostly I don't. What's your death?'

'Mine's a raven.'

'With a name like yours that's not surprising.' But I could see that raven, the blackness of it in a high grey sky as it flapped its wings and grew small in the distance. We left the college together at the end of the day and had coffee at the Greenfields Café in Exhibition Road.

It was a brisk October day, my favourite kind of weather, the time of year that always seems to me a season for new ventures, taking chances, not being too careful. We sat there under an awning while the world and his wife and children walked by and I felt pretty good. I've said that Lenore was striking but some might have called her beautiful; for me there was just that hint of brutality in her mouth and the set of her jaw but she was by anybody's reckoning a good-looking woman. I must admit that I felt a little challenged by her perception of me as a mouse. 'Well,' I said, 'this is a good day for it, don't you think?'

'A good day for what?'

'Anything at all.'

'Yes, here we are today, and some other day you'll sit here with someone else and it'll be a good day for it then as well.'

'Maybe you'll sit here with someone else too. That doesn't make today any less pleasant. My rule is not to piss on a new beginning.'

She shrugged and looked into the middle distance. That's when I made that comment about her walking around in a name out of Edgar Allan Poe and the conversation went on to where she said I was going to make her unhappy. When she asked me if I didn't want to kiss her and make her feel better she wound herself around the question like a serpent around a tree. If we hadn't been sitting at a table at the Greenfields Café it was clear that she'd have wound herself around me.

'Yes,' I said, taking her face in my hands, 'I do want to kiss you and make you feel better.'

'Good,' she said. 'Then we might as well get started on it.' So we did some kissing, then with each other's taste in our mouths we went to South Ken station and took the District Line to Baron's Court. *Mmmmmm?* said the train with the surge of its engine. *Mmmmmm?*

'I know,' I said.

Lenore's flat was up three flights in a house that shook when the trains passed under it. I have followed various bottoms up stairways here and there with varying degrees of expectation; the coming-down, both physical and romantic, was sometimes fast and sometimes slow but Lenore had a fateful bottom, a this-is-it bottom that made me think this was no brief fling.

Her door was black, and when she opened it she switched on pink and blue fluorescent tubes that stuttered into life and gave us more blackness looking at us from the walls of what had once been a living-room and was now a windowless studio with the smells of pigments and linseed oil, damar varnish, turps, and canvas. There was no furniture other than her easel and a tabouret with a crusted palette, jars of brushes, various bottles, and a crumpled paint-rag. There was a canvas on the easel, something dark and unfinished with a dim and spectral figure walking what looked like the lines of a turf maze.

'Don't look at that,' she said. 'It hasn't happened yet.' Other canvases leant against the walls with their backs to me. There were also two or three portfolios, some ethnic cushions on the floor and a couple of cardboard boxes of books and CDs. She picked up one of the discs and went into the bedroom, emerging as the unmistakably modern sound of a clarinet, violin, and piano now issued in something of a serious no-fooling-around nature. I didn't grind my teeth but I clenched them.

'He composed this when he was a prisoner-of-war in Stalag VII in Gorlitz, Silesia,' she informed me.

'Who?' I said.

'Messiaen. This is his *Quartet for the End of Time*. He was inspired by *Revelation X*.' She read from the notes:

And I saw another mighty angel come down from heaven, clothed with a cloud: and a rainbow was upon his head, and his face was as it were the sun, and his feet as pillars of fire . . .

This continued for what seemed a long time, and while she droned on I had a good look at her walls. Almost everywhere she had painted, in purple lines on the black, something reminiscent in style of Goya's *Los Caprichos* but closer in content to Bosch's *Garden of Delights*. She had borrowed his broken eggs on legs, with scenes of her own devising going on inside the eggs. It isn't that they defied description, it's just that I'm not going to describe them. Also in that mural were other creatures composed of autonomous human parts, and the usual compound characters with heads coming out of their bottoms or whatever.

The part of one wall, the one directly ahead as we entered the flat, that was not given up to Lenore's *Garden of Whatever*, rejoiced in two enlargements of Piranesi's Plate VII in my book of his *Prisons* etchings, the one described as *Carcere, with numerous wooden galleries and a drawbridge*. These blow-ups were about 24″ by 36″. The one on the left was the first state, the one on the right the finished etching.

These prints, seen in that size, were overwhelming in the ponderosity of the stone and the improbability of escape on the various bridges, galleries, and stairs all looming in their weight and complexity as the viewer's glance moved upward looking for a way out. The partly raised drawbridge, the feature to which the eye went immediately, sprang from a murkiness on the left and seemed to go nowhere useful on the right.

'Don't tell me,' I said. 'You like Piranesi because you see life as a prison?'

'That goes without saying,' said Lenore, 'but look at State 1.'

I'd seen it often enough in my book: in the first state of the etching the prison seems all light and airy, seems weightless despite its stonework, its winch and tackle, its towers and turrets and bridges all seen through a massive arch.

'Look here,' she said, 'at this staircase on the lefthand side, the one that spirals around the outside of that tower. In the first state he's indicated stairs spiralling right the way up to the top.'

'Yes, what about them?'

'Look at the finished etching: he's obliterated the stairs he'd sketched-in where the first flight of the spiral makes the turn around the tower. Now that flight ends in a hairy shadow where it twists into itself like a wrung-out dishcloth.'

'The spiral continues in the next flight up,' I pointed out.

'Sure it does, but you can't get to it.'

'What are you saying, Lenore?'

'I'm not saying anything – I'm just thinking about that staircase.'

We both thought about it for a while with my hands wandering here and there. Lenore abandoned Piranesi, leered at me pleasantly, took me by the crotch in a hail-fellow-well-met sort of way, and towed me into the bedroom which also had black walls on which the purple drawings continued into scenes more intimate with players genetically more diverse than those in the living-room. 'Let's see,' she said, 'if we can make it round the twist.'

We made it round the twist several times despite the music and the rumble and vibration of the District Line; the bed was a big brass affair that encouraged extravagance and we wanted to make a good impression on each other.

I had noticed, on the little Indian bedside table, *The Complete Poems of Emily Dickinson*, the *I Ching*, Thornton Wilder's *The Bridge of San Luis Rey*, and *Uncle Remus*, by Joel Chandler Harris, a 1917 edition with illustrations by A. B. Frost. I was leafing through this as we lay there close together in a post-coital glow of achievement and camaraderie when Lenore said, 'Will you read to me?'

'Sure,' I said. 'What would you like to hear?'

'*The Wonderful Tar-Baby Story*,' she said. 'You're American so you can do it right.'

'With pleasure,' I said. The bedroom had a window through which came the sounds of evening traffic. I opened the curtains and looked at the October dusk and the golden windows of other houses. Then I got back into bed, switched on a Tiffany-style lamp, arranged Lenore comfortably against me, opened the book, turned to page 7, and began:

One day atter Brer Rabbit fool 'im wid dat calamus root, Brer Fox
went ter wuk en got 'im some tar, en mix it wid some turkentine,
en fix up a contrapshun wat he call a Tar-Baby, en he tuck dish
yer Tar-Baby en he sot 'er in de big road, en den he lay off in
de bushes fer to see wat de news wuz gwineter be . . .

When I'd reached the end, where Brer Rabbit, having tricked
Brer Fox into throwing him into a brier patch, escapes with
the immortal words, 'Bred en bawn in a brier-patch, Brer
Fox – bred en bawn in a brier-patch!', Lenore chuckled
and said, 'That's a pretty good little political allegory, don't
you think?'

'Brer Fox and Brer Rabbit political?'

'I'd have thought it was obvious: Brer Fox is the white
oppressor, Brer Rabbit is the black people, and the Tar-Baby
is the stereotype that was forced upon them. The brier-patch
is the hard place they're used to but they'll get through it and
come out on the other side.'

'Well,' I said, 'one learns something new every day,
doesn't one.'

'If one hangs out with the right people,' said Lenore.

10

ON BUSES

On Wednesday, the day after the dream with the old woman as a black cat, I wanted more than anything else to go looking for Amaryllis although I knew it was better not to be too anxious. Still, I *would* have gone looking for her if I hadn't arranged a couple of weeks before to meet Seamus Flannery for lunch. He teaches at the National Film School and we talk about films a lot along with everything else. We have lunch about once a month and always at Il Fornello, in Southampton Row near Russell Square. Although the restaurant bills itself as Italian the staff are mostly Spanish; they speak Italian when they feel like it but Spanish when the conversation is personal. Juliano and Paco, who mostly serve us, have assigned Seamus, possibly owing to his baldness, the honorific of *Professore*. As I'm younger than he they grant me the distinction of *Dottore*.

Although we usually have the same thing, *Lasagne* for Seamus and *Pizza della Casa* for me, we tend to linger over half-pints of lager while we update each other before ordering.

'What do you think of buses?' Seamus asked me.

'As transportation or as metaphor?' I asked.

'As a sentient system.'

'Say more.'

'Well, you remember the sentient ocean in *Solaris* that responded to thoughts and memories and made them real?'

'Yes.'

'Well, one of my students is working on a screenplay in which London buses respond to the thoughts and feelings of this man who's waiting at a bus stop.'

'That's as good an explanation of their behaviour as any,' I ventured.

'I doubt that the film will ever get made,' said Seamus, 'but the idea of interaction between buses and people is intriguing. I have to say I've sometimes felt there was something more than mechanical going on. Poor old Harold Klein was killed by a 14 bus not all that long ago.'

Harold Klein, an art historian who was seventy-two when he died, had been a mutual friend. 'Harold always had a thing about the 14 bus,' I said. 'It wouldn't surprise me if there came a time when he'd had enough and he stepped out into the road and let the 14 do the job.'

'He used to say that the red of the 14 changed from day to day along with its moods,' said Seamus.

'Speaking of buses,' I said, 'what would you think of a multi-decker made of bamboo and rice paper?'

'Sounds visually interesting.'

I told Seamus about the dream in which I'd first seen Amaryllis.

'You say she wanted you to get on the bus with her?'

'Yes, she beckoned to me.'

'Ah, beckoning! We know about beckoning from the Oliver Onions story, don't we?'

'*The Beckoning Fair One* is the title of the painting I'm working on at the moment.'

'But when she beckoned, you didn't follow.'

'No, I was suddenly afraid, I don't know why.'

Our glasses were empty. We ordered two more half-pints and our lunches. Seamus smoothed down his baldness as he pondered what I'd told him. 'I have no reason to think this, really,' he said, 'but I think you were wise not to get on that bus.'

'You're probably right. I'm glad I didn't.' I said no more about Amaryllis and switched the conversation to *The Bridge of San Luis Rey*. 'I've just read it again for the fourth time,' I said. 'It's a book that seems to say more to me each time. The part where he talks about La Perichole and Uncle Pio, how they were trying "to establish in Peru the standards of the theatres in some Heaven whither Calderón had preceded them" – that always moves me: the idea of humans dedicated to the impossible.'

'Well, it's more or less what makes the world go round, isn't it,' said Seamus, and we tucked into our lasagne and pizza. Was there, I found myself wondering, an impossibility about Amaryllis that I was dedicated to?

Afterwards we went to Virgin in Oxford Street and bought various videos, some of which we'd already taped off TV but which we found, in their pretty boxes, newly desirable. When we parted at the Tottenham Court Road tube station it was late in the afternoon and I still wanted to go looking for Amaryllis but I decided to sleep on it so I went home and had a kip. I dreamt that I was standing on a deserted beach, looking at the sea and listening to the pebbles rattling and clicking as the tide came in. Very pleasant, very restful.

11

HOW CLEVER OF GOD

Thursday morning I looked at *The Beckoning Fair One*, my unfinished painting of the woman turning away from the viewer and moving towards the edge of a cliff. I've done a lot of thinking about the edges of cliffs; there are those made of earth and rock and there are the other kind, the jumping-off places that appear in one's life from time to time. Sometimes the two kinds become one. After a while I took a palette knife and a turpentine-soaked rag and got rid of what was on the canvas and gave myself a new undertone on which to begin again.

The beckoning fair one in the Oliver Onions story was a tantalising ghost who seduced a writer to the point where he went mad; this ghost was exacting in her demands but never to be fully seen, never to be grasped – nothing like the stodgy creature I had painted. All I wanted, really, was the image of a beauty who beckoned but was never attainable, a face that would haunt whoever saw it. I had no intention of leading the viewer over a cliff.

Amaryllis had that air of unattainability. No one, I think, can be possessed by another person, but with her this was more evident than with other women I'd known. That unpossessability was what I wanted to get into my picture. The more I thought about it, the sillier any attempt at a story-telling painting seemed. A straight portrait of that face that now haunted my waking hours as well as my sleep – that was what I wanted to do. Would she be willing to sit for me? Slow down, I told myself. Don't rush it. I seldom take my own advice.

I got through my teaching day uneventfully and decided to go looking for her. Would she be giving a lesson? Was she through for the day? So far our only two venues had been the Science Museum and the Greenfields Café. I closed my eyes and let her image come up like a print in the developing tray. Everything else went away and I saw her face half-turned from me, saw the dear curve of her cheek in the shade of the Greenfields Café awning.

Into the Underground I went, heading for the Eurydice who would lead me out of darkness. Odd – I hadn't realised how much darkness there was in my life until I met Amaryllis. Out I came at South Ken into the sunshine, the tourists and the rest of it. I squeezed through the queue at the bus stop, crossed the road between oncoming cars, strained my eyes for a sight of her, and there she was at the same table we'd sat at three days ago. She grew larger in my eyes and I was astonished at how much more there was to her face than I'd remembered – it was quite complex in its beauty, full of subtleties not noticed at first glance. Perhaps that's why Waterhouse had painted so many similar faces that were all different one from the other. Her T-shirt had words today:

How clever of God to put two holes in the skin of the cat exactly where the eyes are.

Georg Cristoph Lichtenberg

'I've got that one marked in my Penguin Lichtenberg,' I said, 'but it's: "He marvelled at the fact that cats had two holes cut in their fur at precisely the spot where their eyes were."'

'I like mine better,' she said. 'Where've you been the last three nights?'

'The Brass Hotel and Venice and a little shack in the middle of nowhere. I tried to find you but I had no luck.'

She looked a little sceptical at that. Now that I thought of it, I hadn't tried all that hard. I seemed to lack tenacity in my dreams. 'I'm sorry,' I said. 'Were you stuck on that bus all three nights?'

She nodded. 'I had to kick a few people in the face,' she said, 'but I got through it all right and I woke up every time before we got to Finsey-Obay.'

'What's there?'

'Don't know. I've never been.'

'How come you're afraid of it then?'

'I never said I was afraid. Haven't you ever had a bad feeling about some place you've never been?'

'I suppose so. I wish I could have done better with my dreaming. Maybe I'll be fourth time lucky.'

She seemed untroubled by my failure. 'Your heart's in the right place but you're not going to be able to pull me by yourself, I can see that.'

'Have you met anyone who could?'

'No, but I thought you might just have the necessary weirdness in you.'

'Have you always been able to do it?'

'No, it started with the menarche, when I was thirteen. I tuned into my English teacher and pulled him into quite a hot little love scene. The next day he couldn't look me in the eye.'

'Have you done a lot of it since?'

'Let's not lay out our whole histories right now, Peter, OK? Let them open little by little like water flowers as we go on.' She was only twenty-eight, as I found out later, but sometimes she made me feel like a boy receiving instruction from a teacher.

I got the coffee and brought it to the table; while we drank it she was looking into the middle distance and apparently turning something over in her mind. At length she said, 'If I come to your place to spend the night is there somewhere I can sleep other than in your bed with you?'

My heart leapt up. To have her under my roof through the night! 'You take the bed, I'll take the couch.'

'Let's do it the other way around. You should have the more comfortable place to sleep because your part of it's going to be more difficult than mine.'

'You're coming to my place to help me pull you into my dream?'

'That's right.'

'Actually I fall asleep faster and sleep better on the couch. That's my napping place, you see – it's illicit.'

'OK, we'll do it that way then.'

I rested my right elbow on the table with my forearm up as if we were going to arm-wrestle. She did the same and we locked our fingers together. Everything went into freeze-frame; neither of us said anything. After a while I suggested drinks so we headed for the Old Brompton Road. Holding hands and looking forward to dreaming together while sleeping apart.

12

CLIFFS AND EDGES

The Zetland Arms dates from a time well before people walked the streets talking into little telephones. On one of the double doors is a brass plate with plain words:

PERSONS WEARING
SOILED OR DIRTY CLOTHING
ARE NOT WELCOME

Having said that, it offered, once the door was opened, a cool and comforting arrangement of lamps and dimness, smoke and shadows, and from the table where we sat down, a view of daylight through a dark and shapely art nouveau wooden arch and the double-arched glass panels of the doors. The green, gold, and scarlet floral arabesques of the curtains claimed kinship with William Morris; the carpet had heard of Kelim. Etched glass mirrors and machines of many dancing colours varied the background while a juke-box maintained a modest thump-and-whine continuo to the gentle prevailing hubbub. Some of the figures were silhouettes, others were in chiaroscuro; sometimes a hand came out of the shadows into the light; sometimes half a face.

On the wall an old clock, once ticking and tocking courtesy of the Brewery, Reading, looked down indulgently, having stopped at midnight unknown years ago.

The only vacant table was close to a clean-shaven old man whose nose looked as if it had been broken more than once. He was wearing pin-stripe trousers with red braces, a short-sleeved collarless white shirt, and well-shined black shoes. The braces were the kind that button into the trousers. Tattoos on both arms honoured Mother and the Union Jack. He was nursing a pint while an old bull terrier bitch lay near his feet and snored. An empty willow-pattern bowl was near her head. 'Her name's Queenie,' he said. 'Born here, bred here, worked hard all her life.'

'Doing what?' I asked him.

'Watching and waiting.'

'For what?'

'Things to get better.'

'That's not an easy job.'

Queenie growled a little in her sleep.

'She's worn out,' said her master. 'Bloody yuppies.' He subsided into his pint.

'Bitter?' I said.

'With good reason,' he said.

'I meant your pint. What're you drinking?'

'John Smith, same as Queenie.'

'What'll you have?' I asked Amaryllis.

'Whatever you're having,' she said.

I got a pint of bitter and a large whisky for the old man and a pint for Queenie and a pint and a large whisky each for Amaryllis and me.

'Thank you,' said the old man. 'What's the occasion?'

'This lady is drinking with me for the first time.'

'Well done you!' He raised his glass to us. 'May it be the first of many. If God had meant people to stay sober he wouldn't have created malt and hops.' He poured Queenie's drink into her bowl and at the sound she awoke, sighed, and began to lap it up. 'You don't look like a yuppie,' said her master kindly.

'Actually I'm not all that young and I don't seem to be moving upward.'

'I'll drink to that,' he said, and raised his glass again. Queenie stopped lapping and growled.

Amaryllis seemed preoccupied. 'See you in my dreams,' I said. That got a smile, then she drank about half her whisky and began to cry into the rest of it.

'What is it?' I said. 'What's the matter?'

She wiped her eyes, blew her nose, finished the whisky, started the beer, and reached for my hand. 'I always spoil everything,' she said.

'What have you spoiled?'

With her free hand she made a wide gesture as if to sweep about half the room out of the way. 'Everything I've touched so far.'

'Are you going to tell me more?'

'Not yet. You haven't got my last name or my address or phone number and I've told you almost nothing about me because I'm afraid of what we're getting into. I've tried to find others who could go with me in both lives but it's never worked out. Maybe it will with you but I'm terribly afraid of failing again if I try to go too fast and I don't want to get on that bus without you. What scares me is that I think maybe the dream life is the main one and this other one is just what fills in the time in between. Are you with me?'

'Amaryllis, I love you.' I hadn't meant to say that, it just slipped out. I'd been in love with her since I first saw her at the Balsamic bus stop.

'Oh, Peter,' she said, and grabbed my hand and kissed it. 'Don't love me yet, not so soon – maybe not ever. If it happens too fast it'll end too soon with a big drop, like walking off the edge of a cliff, when . . .'

'When what?'

'When you see me as I really am.'

'And how are you really?'

'Not to be depended on, and maybe you're not either. Some people need to be in love and I think you're one of them. So am I, but after a while we'll both fall out of love, and if I do before you do it'll be a terrible drop for you.'

'I'm not going to fall out of love with you, Amaryllis.'

'You'll love me for ever, will you?'

Lenore came to mind and I had no immediate answer.

Amaryllis, reading my face, said, 'Have you ever promised to love anyone for ever?'

'Yes, but it wasn't the same.'

'How was it different?'

'In too many ways for me to explain. Amaryllis, don't cross-examine me like this – you can feel how I feel, I know you can.'

'I think you probably feel the way I do: I love being in love but I don't know what love is. Is it like fireworks that you see in the sky, then the sky goes dark again and there's nothing but the smell of gunpowder? I've never stuck around long enough to find out what comes next. Have you?'

'How I've been in the past isn't how I am now.'

'How are you now?'

'In love with you. You're different from anyone I've known before and that difference has changed me. Whether you believe that or not I can't alter the way I feel, so we might as well relax about it and just go on as we've been doing. When there's no more ground under my feet I'll do the big drop or whatever.'

'Have you ever given anyone that big drop?'

'Wasn't it you that said we should let our histories open little by little like water flowers?'

'You've answered my question. People do it to each other all the time. The frog said he'd turn into a handsome prince if the princess kissed him but the princess said she'd rather have a talking frog.'

'You have dashed my hops.'

'So how do we get through the hours from now until dream-time?'

'Hang on,' I said, 'we're empty.' I stood up to get refills but as I did so the old man appeared with two pints and two large whiskies on a tray which he set on the table.

'Happy days to you and the young lady!' he said, raising his glass as he sat down again.

'And to you and Queenie!' I said as we raised our glasses to him. I noticed that he hadn't got refills for himself and I feared that I'd potlatched him into a gesture he couldn't afford.

'When I tuned in to you I wasn't thinking ahead,' said Amaryllis. 'I was desperate for someone to connect with, I had a good feeling about you, I pulled you into my dream and here you are up to your neck in my weirdness.'

'It takes two to make this particular weirdness, Amaryllis. I'm not sorry to be part of it. Are you sorry you pulled me?'

'Actually, no.'

'There,' I said, 'see how easy it is to get the bullshit out of the way?'

'You Americans – so direct.'

'Now then, about getting through the hours: we can have something to eat and then go to my place and watch a video until it's late enough to go to sleep. Or we could go right to my place and order something in and watch two videos before bedtime. Or maybe you'd let me do some sketches of you?'

'Sketches for what?'

'For a painting of you.'

'Maybe that's a good idea – if you look at me long enough you'll stop seeing the Pre-Raphaelite nymph. Let's go to your place and order a pizza and do sketches and a video until it's time to get started on the dreamwork.'

While we were finishing our drinks the old man picked up Queenie's empty bowl and she awoke with a grunt. 'I'd better get her home while she can still walk,' he said. 'It was nice meeting you; good luck to you both.'

'And to you,' we both said as Queenie lurched to her feet and padded after him into the unblinking sunlight. The way the two of them walked made me think there was nobody waiting at home for him and Queenie.

13

NICE ONE

Amaryllis wanted to see the studio before we did anything else. She walked all around it like a cat sniffing out a new home and as she did so I was newly aware of the smells of my workplace which was my main living-place: turpentine; linseed oil; damar varnish; canvas; gesso; hardboard; the new wood of stretchers; the paint on my palette; the musty cushions on my napping couch; the evaporated whisky dregs in unwashed glasses; mouldy cups of coffee; and the pong of solitary hours.

She opened the doors to the balcony, went out and had a good look up and down the street where the only action was that of the builders on the scaffolding two doors down and the sound of their drills and Capitol Radio with the revenant voice of Mick Jagger singing 'I Can't Get No Satisfaction'. She glanced up at the sky in a weatherwise manner and I wondered if she had a knotted handkerchief for summoning the winds.

She came back in and pulled canvases out of the rack and studied them critically. Ordinarily I'm moderately arrogant but seeing the paintings through her eyes I wondered if I was as good as I needed to be. After a while she said, 'There's a lot of darkness in your paintings.'

'There's a lot of darkness in everything.'

She read notes that I'd written to myself and pinned to the corkboard. There were two or three pen-and-ink sketches for the version of *The Beckoning Fair One* that I'd scraped.

'She's moving to the edge of a cliff?' she asked me.

'That's what used to be on the canvas that's blank now.'

'Why'd you scrape it?'

'It wasn't right.'

'Wasn't right for her to go to the edge of the cliff?'

'Wasn't the right woman.'

'Who'll the right woman be?'

'I'll know her when I see her.' The late-afternoon light was gilding her with faint music and magic spells. 'Sit on that stool, Amaryllis, and let me draw you.'

She sat on the stool and I pinned some large sheets of cartridge paper to a board, put the board on the easel, and began to draw with conté sanguine. She looked at me and I looked at her and found myself understanding John William Waterhouse as I never had before. She'd been wrong to say that I'd stop seeing the Pre-Raphaelite nymph: his nymphs, his sirens, his tragic women of myth and story – they were each and every one a beckoning fair one; their beauty and their melancholy and their sadness beckoned the viewer to follow unquestioningly wherever they might lead him. 'Come with us,' said those lovely faces, those glances ardent and wistful. 'Come with us to the heart of the mystery.'

All of the nymphs and sirens and tragic women came and went in Amaryllis's face, and sometimes there flickered there that face all thin and pale and haggard that I'd seen when she pulled me into her dream. I made sketch after sketch, never trying for finish but searching in each for whatever

I'd missed in the one before. The conté crayon, rasping and tapping the paper as it stroked, seemed guided not by me but by what I looked at – I simply held it lightly while it drew with unerring mastery. She took a five-minute rest every twenty minutes, then we continued.

As I tried to possess her with my eyes and my drawings I recognised that I was giving myself up to the idea of *The One*, the woman who would be all that I ever wanted, would satisfy all longing and all desire, would be the perfect companion and lover for ever. But of course there is no for ever for us mortals; time goes on without us. 'Oh Galuppi, Baldassaro, this is very sad to find!' I thought, trying to recall the Browning poem. But all that came to me was, 'What of soul was left, I wonder, when the kissing had to stop?' Little by little the afternoon slanted into evening but in the dusk I saw new things until the light and I had nothing more to give.

Amaryllis switched on a lamp and came to look at the drawings. There were twelve and she examined each one carefully. As she leant towards me I smelled her hair and closed my eyes. How could she smell so much like a country childhood? I kissed the top of her head. 'You,' she said. She put her hand on my neck, pulled my face to hers, and kissed me for a long time. She tasted like sunwarmed wild strawberries, the blue skies and the high kites of long ago. I hoped it was a hello kiss and not a goodbye one; I was always uncertain with her. 'I'm hungry,' she said.

So we ordered pizza. When the delivery man arrived on his motor scooter I was suddenly filled with pity for him that he had no Amaryllis. I tipped him £2.00 and he looked at me suspiciously, the dark face of the world indifferent to my happiness.

The drawing session had been thirsty work and the pepperoni cried out for Chianti which I happened to have a few bottles of. As we ate and drank it seemed to both of us that the evening was shaping nicely. I couldn't remember a time when I had drawn so well or felt so good; I wondered if I'd ever draw that well and feel that good again. Happiness can be unsettling, like catching a baby that someone has thrown out of a window.

After the pizza we went to the sitting-room for video time. Amaryllis ranged the shelves, considering and rejecting various films until she settled on *Notorious*. 'This is the one I want,' she said. 'Every time I watch it I'm so afraid that they won't get away in the end.'

'I've seen this film many times,' I said, 'and so far they've always made it; after all, the taxi's right there ready to go – it isn't as if they have to hang about waiting for a bus.'

She leant against me briefly. 'I don't take anything for granted any more.' She shook her head. 'Ingrid Bergman was so adorable in this one and now she's dead of cancer.'

'Cary Grant's dead too, and Claude Rains; Alfred Hitchcock as well,' I said. 'It's mainly a dead-people film but there's a lot of life in it.'

'Ghosts,' said Amaryllis. 'And yet sometimes when I'm watching this film I think it's realer than I am.'

'Feeling unreal is part of reality.' I gave her a little hug, just with one arm, delicately. There was a bottle of grappa around so we had some of that to cut the pizza grease, then feeling well refreshed we settled down on the couch and arranged ourselves cosily to watch the film.

'So many things were against her from the beginning,' said Amaryllis. 'She couldn't help it that her father was a

Nazi, and because she was loyal to the USA the American government used her as a spy. Fathers!'

'You have father problems?'

She didn't answer that. 'And Cary Grant,' she said, 'why did he have to be so cold when you could see she was ready to fall in love with him right from the start? She was so vulnerable!'

The Chianti and the grappa and the smell of Amaryllis's hair were making me drowsy and contented. 'I was thinking about how they get from one scene to the next,' I said. 'There's no long drive to the airport, no queuing-up to check in. Right away they're in a plane and they look out of the window and there's Rio. Cut to an aerial view of a broad avenue and next they're in a restaurant. Think of all the time and energy they've saved! No wonder they can deal with danger better than the rest of us.'

'It's the in-between moments that I miss,' said Amaryllis, fitting herself into the crook of my arm and snuggling comfortably against me. 'We'll never know if their hands touched on the way to the airport or if they exchanged a look that had their whole future in it: no words, just a destiny-look that made her not give up on him no matter what happened.'

Previous viewings notwithstanding, the two of us couldn't breathe easily until Cary Grant and Ingrid Bergman got into the taxi that took them to safety. We both liked Claude Rains and felt sorry for him but he had to play the part Ben Hecht wrote for him – it was just his rotten luck that as a villain who'd blotted his copybook with the other Nazis he wasn't likely to survive the closing frames of the film.

By then it was about quarter to two and we both felt as if sleep might come soon after we closed our eyes. 'Wait,' said Amaryllis, 'before we go to bed I want to look at the moon.'

'Is there one tonight?'

'There must be – I feel moony, I feel a full moon looking down. Can we see it from the balcony?'

'Depends on whether it's rising or setting.'

I followed her up to the studio and we went out on to the balcony. There it was, a full moon riding low in a pale sky over the common, so sharp and clear that I could almost see the craters. I felt moony too, felt the pull of it and the surge of the spring tide. 'Yes!' said Amaryllis, smacking the balustrade with her hand, and we went down to the bedroom floor again.

'May I use your toothbrush?' she said.

'It would be my pleasure.' I had new spare toothbrushes but I didn't want to pass up any kind of intimacy. I gave her a T-shirt to sleep in.

'This one doesn't say anything,' she said.

'Maybe it'll have something to say tomorrow morning.' I remembered, then, that I hadn't put fresh sheets on the bed and I was going to do it but she stopped me.

'That's OK,' she said. 'Your smell will help me into your dream. As soon as you're ready I'll show you a way to get started.'

When I'd organised the couch in the studio where I'd spend the night she came and sat beside me on it. We were both wearing only T-shirts and knickers and her left leg was touching my right leg. 'Probably,' she said, 'it'll help if you use a focusing device.'

'Such as what?' The hairs on her leg were golden in the lamplight.

'You know how to make a Möbius strip?'

'Yes.'

'Make one, not too big, with a slider.'

I got what I needed, then I returned and put my right leg back where it had been. I took a sheet of A4 yellow paper and cut a lengthwise strip about a quarter-inch wide. On this I put a paper slider like a movable belt loop which I marked with a red X. I gave the long strip a twist and taped the ends together to make a Möbius strip on which the slider could move freely.

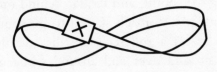

'Right,' she said. 'The thing is to move your head out of its ordinary busy-busy mode and make a clear space for things to happen in. I'll go to my bed now and you lie down here. Look at the Möbius strip while you go around it with the slider. You're going to be pulling me into your dream so you should have me in your mind's eye while you're sliding the Möbius. Easy does it, just float with it, OK?'

'OK.'

'You're going to do it, I can feel it in you.' She kissed me with what was unmistakably a destiny kiss. 'See you in your dream,' she whispered.

'What if one of us is still awake while the other one's asleep?'

'If we're tuned in right that won't happen. Trust me, I'm a weirdo.'

She left me to it then. I slid my Möbius while I let her face come to me. I saw her half-turned away from me, saw the sweet curve of her cheek and held it lightly in my mind's eye while I looked fixedly at the red X on the Möbius slider. I moved it around the twist and watched it change sides while the curve of her cheek stayed with me. Around it went. And again. And again. I closed my eyes, seeing her face more and more clearly as the slider moved round the twist. 'Amaryllis!' I said. 'Balsamic! Finsey-Obay!'

I thought I might faint but I didn't. My head went . . . *wide* – that's the only way I can describe it. Immensities of space all around me. Then it went *long* – space far, far in front of me, dwindling to a point, and far, far behind me to another vanishing point. My stomach started to go somewhere and I stayed with it on a rollercoaster ride, dizzily swooping and twisting, up and over and around while being pulled inside out and passing through myself and the manyness that constituted me: faces I'd long forgotten, voices I'd never hear again, sighs of love and groans of regret; streets of night and day under moons, under lamps, under rain and longing. Then I was back in the wide space and things quieted down enough for me to go to the bathroom and vomit.

I came back exhausted, fell asleep and found myself on the Finsey-Obay bus, climbing the stairs to the upper deck behind Amaryllis. This time she was wearing only a T-shirt, no knickers.

She turned and smiled down at me. 'Get a good glim?' she said.

'Lovely. Much appreciated. Are you Scottish?'

'Not if you take your time. Speaking of glims, I don't think we should use the d-word any more.'

'The d-word?' My mind was not entirely on what she was saying.

'You know – what we're in now; what happens when you're asleep and you have rapid eye movement.'

'Oh, you mean . . .'

'Best not to say that word any more, it can make you wake up too soon. Let's call this a glim, which is what it is, really: a glimpse of this and that. OK?'

'Sometimes glim means lamp.'

'Well, lamps throw light on things, don't they. Anyhow, well done you, this is the first time you've done the glim and pulled me. I noticed that it took you a while. Was it hard for you?'

'Piece of cake. I'll probably get into it faster next time.'

'That's the ticket. I think I should tell you that Amaryllis is also the name of the family of herbs that belladonna belongs to − deadly nightshade.'

'Is that a warning?'

'Would a warning discourage you?'

'No. If the going gets tough I can always throw up.'

'You're a stayer, that's good.'

By now we'd gone far beyond the level of any ordinary upper deck; the spiral stairs we were on seemed to have no upper limit in this bamboo and paper tower; the bus moved silently ahead, and as we climbed the wind rippled the paper and our shadows rose and fell in the fluttering light of candles that swung in a bamboo chandelier. The candles and bamboo had a Christmas smell. So frail, that bus! I kept expecting it to fall over and burn.

'Is there someone behind you?' said Amaryllis.

I turned and looked, and there was Hastings trying to see around me so he could look up Amaryllis's T-shirt. I put my foot in his face and shoved. He fell with a tremendous amount of thumping and bumping, and only then did I see that his fall had knocked four or five others off the stairs.

The thumping and bumping continued for a long time, then there was silence.

'You're a take-charge guy, Peter,' said Amaryllis. 'I like that.'

'Thanks, but when I pushed that bloke off the stairs he took quite a few others with him. I hope they weren't hurt.'

'Don't worry about it – if they were here they were up to no good.'

'How do you know that?'

'From experience; I've gone this route before.'

'What about the one right behind me? What was he doing here?'

'Hey, remember whose glim this is. No knickers was your idea and so was Hastings.'

'Oh, you know him, do you?'

'We've gone out a few times.'

'I'm surprised you didn't pick him for a companion on your night journeys, or did he outlive his glimfulness so you moved on to me?'

'I think the bus is stopping,' she said. 'You're a good glimmer – I've never been able to do that. Let's get off while we can.' She came back down the stairs, putting a hand on my shoulder and sending waves of warmth down the whole length of me.

When we got off the bus it was very dim and foggy but I was able to make out the marquee of the Brass Hotel. There was nothing else in sight, nothing at all around it – just the Brass Hotel shining like a beacon. The doorman was a bull-necked Prussian sort; he looked like Erich von Stroheim. He tipped his brass hat to Amaryllis and said good evening while ignoring me. She returned his greeting and went to the reception desk. 'Room 318,' she said. Without a word the brassy woman gave her the key.

'Do you come here often?' I said.

She turned her face to me and there were tears in her eyes. 'Please, Peter,' she said very softly, 'be kind.' Several uncredited extras waited for the lift with us, and with them my uncle, Stanley Diggs, whom I hadn't seen since I was a boy. He had the look of an unaccompanied husband. Where was Aunt Florence? I wondered. No one paid any attention to Amaryllis's casual attire. We watched the indicator as the lift descended; the doors opened, more uncredited extras came out, and with them Lenore. She was wearing something black and slinky and she looked right through me and passed on without a word. I couldn't believe I was seeing her. Right behind her came the old woman in her black-cat outfit. Raising her right hand, she made a circle with thumb and second finger and peeped at me through it, then shook her head and moved on.

'What is this,' I said, 'old home week?'

'What?' said Amaryllis.

'Sorry, I often mutter to myself.'

'You seem a million miles away,' she said, 'and I need you to be with me.' She took my hand and leant against me. 'I know all this seems strange to you but are we in it together?'

I was trying to pay attention but my mind was busy with Uncle Stanley and Lenore and the old woman. What were they doing at the Brass Hotel? I stole a glance at Uncle Stanley but he was studiously avoiding eye contact.

'*Are* we?' said Amaryllis.

'Are we what?'

'In it together?'

'In what, Amaryllis? What is it that we're in?'

'Whatever it is. Do you always have to know what's happening?'

I thought about that for a moment with the warmth of her pressing against me. 'I guess not. And yes, we're in it together.' Who else is in it with us? I wondered.

'This is such a nice one, Peter,' she said, moving her face towards mine. I realised suddenly that she no longer looked like the thin and haggard dream self I had seen the first time; she now looked the same as in the unglim.

'Nice what?' I said.

'What it is.' She stopped my mouth with hers and kissed me as if her life depended on it. She tasted as I remembered: sunwarmed wild strawberries, the blue skies and the high kites of childhood.

When we left the lift at the third floor Uncle Stanley got out too. He still hadn't given any sign of recognition which wasn't surprising really – the last time he saw me I was still in short trousers. He was just behind us in the corridor and stopped at 317, the room next to ours.

In 318 the brass-coloured curtains and chair and bedspread had brass threads in the fabric. There was a brass TV, and on the brass walls were framed prints of brass doorknobs, locks, keys, and other brassmongery. The whole room leant towards me brazenly. The bed was brass but the mattress wasn't. Amaryllis bounced on it a couple of times, then she said, 'See if there's anybody outside our door.'

I opened the door and looked out. I saw no one but the door of 317 clicked as it was closed from the inside. When I turned, Amaryllis's T-shirt was coming off over her head. As I'd half-noted in the bus, there was surprisingly more to her than there was in clothes. As I got my things off I saw crumpled words on the T-shirt that lay on the floor. 'What does it say?' I said.

'*Unnatural practices yes*,' she murmured, and fitted her nakedness to mine. Through the brass walls from 317 came the sounds of laughter and rhythmical bedsprings.

14

MEMORY'S ARROW

Time's arrow, we are told, is a one-way thing. I've certainly never found any way to roll it back so that I could change my actions and the consequences of them. Memory's arrow, like the needle of a compass too close to a lodestone, spins in all directions. And lodestones are more frequent than pot-holes on the streets of Used-To-Be. Regret, some of them are called; Shame, Sorrow, and Stupidity: I have many to choose from. Some of the lodestones, of course, are called Pleasure or even Happiness but as Memory's arrow spins it points more often in other directions.

This is a warning: bear in mind as you read my story that I am not an uninvolved author constructing a narrative; no, indeed. I'm in this not only up to my neck but over my head and I'm telling it my way. As people, when they become friends, take a little while to open up, so I too have some reserve, some reticence – in short, don't expect me to spill my guts all at once. If you want to stay with me, fine; if not, go with God. Or whatever you go with when you go.

Seen from the cliffs at Beachy Head, the sea was grey and dimpled, far, far below us like a leaden porridge slowed by distance, advancing in sluggish small wavelines to the base of the cliffs. The newly risen sun, impartially illuminating a fan of mawkishly mild strato-cumulus clouds, offered nothing but the blank whiteness of its disc. The tiny lighthouse, red-and-white striped, was like something out of a Christmas cracker, not to be taken seriously as a warning to mariners. *Look at me*, it said. *Look how puny I am, how much of a toy. How can I possibly help anybody in the leaden porridge of the sea or on the high chalk cliffs?*

A sign by the phone box said:

The Samaritans
ALWAYS THERE
DAY AND NIGHT
Phone 735555 or 0345 909090

Perched on the sign was a meditation of crows. I thought they might sing 'Hit That Jive, Jack' but they avoided eye contact, said nothing, and flew away. 'Not ravens,' I said to Lenore, 'crows.'

In the phone box was a card with its number and location:

01323 721807
Nr Beachy Head P. H.
Eastbourne
East Sussex BN20 7YA

On the shelf in the phone box was a stack of paperbacks, all of them *Notes from a Friend, A Quick and Simple Guide to Taking Charge of Your Life* by Anthony Robbins. Riffling the pages I happened on some word lists for transforming 'Old Boring Words' into 'New Exciting Words'. 'Interesting' became 'amazing'; 'awake' became 'energised'; 'cool' became 'outrageous'. I turned to the beginning. *Lesson One* was FEELING OVERWHELMED ... HOW TO TURN IT AROUND. *Lesson Two* was THERE ARE NO FAILURES. On the flyleaf Ted Danson, Christauria Welland Akong, and Arnold Schwarzenegger were quoted praising the book highly. A little gift card pasted there bore the holograph message:

> The fact that you're alive means
> that someone cares about you.
>
> Merry Christmas
> From
> A Friend

'The fact that I'm alive only means that I'm not dead,' said Lenore. 'It doesn't mean that anyone cares about me.'

'*I* care about you.'

'OK, but that's not what's keeping me alive. And look at all the billions and trillions of us walking around being alive, billions too many of us. Do you really think that someone cares about every one of us?'

'I very much doubt it.'

A little brown dog frolicked ahead of us in transports of joy; a black Labrador urged caution as we walked through the sodden grass towards the cliff's edge. This was New Year's Day 1994. The weather was mild; there'd been some drizzle but it had cleared and the morning now presented that special kind of daylight one sees on New Year's day after having been up all night: a different country, that daylight.

Lenore and I had left my house at 06:15. It was cold, it was dark; the night gleamed with blackness in which a white moon, three days past the full, said, *This is your life*. Lenore's Citroën 2CV, sporting a several-years-old cerulean-blue paint job, seemed an inadequate vehicle for the imperious spirit of its driver: the heater didn't work very well, the valves and pistons seemed not entirely able to achieve compression, the clutch had lost its grip, and the whole machine rattled and shook and protested the pathetic fallacy of its lot. Lenore drove as if hacking her way through the jungle with a machete. I was the navigator, I had a little torch, I had an atlas, I was in love; all things seemed possible; I could find anything from Land's End to John o' Groat's and I had provided ham-and-cheese sandwiches and a thermos of tea.

Wandsworth Bridge Road was empty; the street lamps all pointed to the future. The Shell station just before the bridge glowed saffron and scarlet like a temple at the gates of Night. Coming off the bridge we saw the netted sparkle of lights in the blackness looking like Los Angeles in a thriller.

We got on to the A214 and went through Tooting Bec on the way to Croydon. At 06:25 it had a Marie-Celeste look, abandoned beneath its Christmas decorations. Indoors the townspeople slept or lay awake, made love or vomited up the remains of the evening while we outdoors moved through the night towards a new dawn. Always the street lamps offered perspectives receding to vanishing points. And each point we passed through was a vanishing point for someone up ahead.

'Do you feel yourself always vanishing and reappearing?' I asked Lenore.

'I'm always vanishing; I'm not sure whether I actually reappear. On New Year's Eve I can feel the next year coming with some kind of a self to cover my vanishment.'

'A new self?'

'I don't aim that high. Any kind of self will do; used is OK – two or three careful owners. Whatever.'

I live in a state of surprise much of the time; things others take for granted suddenly amaze me. Moving towards the ever-receding vanishing point I was struck by the frailty of what humans have put together like something out of a box: houses; shops; roads; street lamps; trains and railway stations; aeroplanes and airports. I imagined a gigantic foot stepping on it. Crunch. Of course film-makers imagine that all the time, and build monsters on to the feet.

'Oi!' said Lenore. 'Mr Navigator!'

'What?'

'We're going through Tooting Bec. What happens next?'

'Mitcham, then Croydon.' Like an animated line on a TV map we advanced through Croydon where a silver four-propeller-engine aeroplane was mounted in front of a floodlit deco building: Airport House. BOOKING HALL, said the entrance marquee; WEDDING FUNCTION.

'Do you think the wedding function is happening right now?' I said.

'It's a vampire wedding,' said Lenore. 'They have to clear out before the sun comes up.'

The vampire wedding at Croydon remains a vivid memory for me – the happy couple sinking their teeth into each other's necks, the guests all drinking (?) too much and the child vampires dancing with their elders as the band played 'The Transylvania Polka'. A lot of the vampire kids would be grown up by now.

After Purley we got on to the A22 through Kenley, Whyteleafe, and Caterham. I think it was on our way out of Caterham that we hit a stretch of unlit road. 'Dark roads always seem fateful to me,' said Lenore.

'In what way?' I said.

'I don't know – just the unknown making itself visible.'

Godstone and East Grinstead came and went as the sky lightened to the most delicate cerulean. *General Amnesty*, said the sky. *All sins forgiven. Clean slate.*

I feel young, said the Citroën 2CV. *I can do this, I can make it to Beachy Head.*

'I wonder if the vampire couple will still be together a year from now,' said Lenore.

'I guess they take it one night at a time,' I said. 'Look, the morning star.' We pulled over briefly for a morning-star kiss. 'Am I making you unhappy?' I said.

'There's a period of natural immunity in these things,' she said. 'Reality comes later; we haven't got there yet.'

I remember inky-black trees against that wonderful paling cerulean sky, very Edmund Dulac. Looking at that sky one could believe in flying carpets, jinn in bottles, even an utterly new year. It's difficult to force remembered images into chronological sequence. Those crows on the Samaritans sign at Beachy Head, I see them often.

Coming though Eastbourne there was definitely a classic rosy-fingered dawn lighting up the clouds on our left, while on our right the drifting dark smudges of all the accumulated dawns before this one reluctantly quitted the stage and a few gulls, like aerial extras, completed the scene.

We were climbing then, with lots of sky all around us and was that – yes, it was – the sea, just a greyness, a flatness, a Here-I-amness. We parked at the Beachy Head Countryside Centre, a brown national-park-looking place, THE FAMILY WELCOME, Full menu served all day, 11:30 a.m. to 10:00 p.m.

With our sandwiches and thermos of tea we made our way

71

to the view of the white cliffs and the toy lighthouse and the grey and kelpy-looking strand between while the sea, grey and dimpled, moved far, far below us like a leaden porridge slowed by distance, advancing in sluggish small wavelines to the base of the cliffs. The joyful little brown dog frolicked ahead of us while the black Labrador continued to urge caution. Reaching the edge of the grass the little brown dog flung himself over headfirst and we were afraid to look but it was not the end of him because he reappeared laughing so it had not after all been an edge of no return.

That was six years ago, and when my mind goes back to that dawn it gives me the vampire wedding, the leaden porridge of the sea, and that meditation of crows.

15

FROM HERE ON OUT TO WHERE?

Sitting naked on our bed in the Brass Hotel Amaryllis said, 'How is it with us now, Peter?' Her voice was very small. She was such a changeable creature, at one moment a confident enchantress and the next touchingly unsure of herself. In the golden light of the brass bedlamps she sat on the rumpled brass-coloured sheets, hugging herself. Her ribs seemed childlike and pathetic. She had a tattoo on her belly just above her pubic hair, a blue yin-yang symbol.

'How do you mean?' I said.

'I mean, are you with me? I don't want to be alone any more.'

This is a glim, I was thinking. What will she say in real life? Is real life as real as this? 'You're not alone any more,' I said.

'Why? Because you've slept with me?'

'We slept together because you tuned in to me and I tuned in to you and now we're . . .' Be careful, I said to myself – don't leap without looking.

'We're what, Peter?'

'Together.'

'For how long?'

So small she looked, so sweet and vulnerable. 'From here on out,' I said.

'From here on out to where?' When she said that I saw a dark road empty under an evening sky, pine woods on either side. Was that a very large ramshackle-looking black cat?

'Wherever,' I said.

'Do you mean that? Doesn't it sound crazy to you? You really don't know me at all.'

'Yes, I mean it. I know it sounds crazy and I don't know you at all but there it is.'

'Can I believe you? It isn't easy to be sure.'

'Believe me, you can be sure.' My mouth kept running ahead of me while I struggled to keep up.

'I don't know you at all, really. I don't always get it right when I tune in. Maybe you're not as alone as I am, maybe you've already got somebody.'

'I've got nobody but you, Amaryllis.'

'But it happened so fast,' she said very softly, almost more to herself than to me.

'Well, after all, things move faster in a . . .'

'Peter, don't say the wrong word!'

'Dream,' I said as I woke up. 'Nobody but you, Amaryllis.'

16

LISTING

I looked at my watch: 03:42 and I felt as if I'd been dropped
from a tall building. Reality! Very confusing. The glim I'd
just woken out of seemed realer than anything else that had
happened between Amaryllis and me but then . . . I keep
trying to find the best description of reality for myself –
a practical working description is what I want, nothing
philosophical or metaphysical. It isn't, for example, a level
plain; it's full of dips and gullies, with here and there a ha-ha
on the private lands. But really it's different things at different
times. Amaryllis – and I closed my eyes to bring her back – had
in that glim given me whatever was her reality in those present
moments. It didn't matter that she was full of unknowns, a
mystery to me. I had the taste of her in my mouth and in
my mind.

Was she awake too? I wanted to look at her, asleep or
awake. I went down to the bedroom and stood at the closed
door, hesitating. I imagined her waking up and wanting to be
alone with her recall of the glim. I turned away and went up
to the studio, sat down at my desk and moved the computer
keyboard out of the way. It was time to make a list and I
wanted to do it in handwriting so as not to miss any clues

my hand might offer. I took a sheet of yellow A4 and a black fibre-tip pen; for a heading I wrote BALSAMIC:

* GLIM 1 – The queue at the Balsamic bus stop. Amaryllis looks at me, gets on Finsey-Obay bus. I wake up. Who were the others in the queue?

* FIRST REAL-LIFE MEETING – Science Museum, at the Klein-bottle display. We go for coffee in Exhibition Road. When she leaves I ask how to get in touch with her. She says, 'At the Balsamic?'

* QUESTION – Is the Balsamic bus stop there in the glimworld even when nobody's glimming it?

* GLIM 2 – The Brass Hotel. The receptionist laughs at me.

* GLIM 3 – Venice. Commissario Brunetti can't help me.

* GLIM 4 – The shack in the pine woods. The old woman posing as a black cat says, 'There is a bomb in Gilead.'

* GLIM 5 – On spiral stairs in Finsey-Obay bus. Looking up at her bare bottom. I kick Hastings and others down stairs. Stop at the Brass Hotel. Lovemaking in Room 318. T-shirt says, '*Unnatural practices yes*'. Amaryllis anxious about what's between us. I say the d-word and wake up. Why did I say the d-word?

* KLEIN BOTTLES – Metaphorical connection? (I noticed that I had some difficulty in writing Klein; the letters ran together in an ill-formed way.)

* QUESTION: She said Hastings on the bus was my idea. Maybe he was, but what she said when we talked about it – was that coming from her or from me? Maybe when I'm doing the glim I set up the location and the situation but what develops depends on who and what is in the glim.

* HASTINGS – Probably he and Amaryllis have been lovers. Do I care? It seems not. I wonder who else was in her life before we. Or still is.
* QUESTION – Amaryllis is sleeping in my bed. When she wakes up are we going to take up where we left off in the glim or will things be as they were before the glim?

I went to see if she was still asleep. She wasn't in my bed. She wasn't in the studio or on the balcony. She wasn't in the bathroom or the kitchen. She was nowhere in the house. The night was gone, the day was here; the tube trains were running and the trees on the common were swaying in the cool of a morning that was going to turn hot very soon. Some birds were twittering in a half-hearted way, as if they were working to rule. At that time of day I always have the feeling that if you gave reality a good kick the scenery would shake.

17

LATE LAST NIGHT

She hadn't left a note to say where and when she wanted to meet next. She *was* skittish, after all. Surely that wasn't asking too much of her, a next-morning word or two?

Thursday was here again, and the last thing I wanted to do was go in to the college; I was dreading what Hastings might bring in this time. 'Pull yourself together,' I said to my face in the mirror. So I did and I went.

I'd asked them to see what they could do with images from glims but only a few had anything to show me. The others said they didn't glim – which was nonsense because everybody glims – or they hadn't been able to recall anything. Hastings didn't turn up at all. Of the five who brought in work only Cindy Ackerman had something that interested me. She'd covered a large sheet of paper with scribbled notes and diagrams that weren't actually Klein bottles but suggested them.

'What've we got here?' I asked her.

'I'm not sure,' she said. 'The dream was like an animation that kept reiterating the idea of something that passes through itself and that's about all I can say.'

I glanced at a few lines of her notes and read:

Then and there and now and here and she and I and not and was and then and now and here and there and was and was and not and was . . .

The words made my stomach churn a little as if I were on a fairground ride. 'Have you been to the Science Museum lately?' I said.

'No. Why?'

'What you've got here looks like something you might have seen at one of the exhibits.'

'No, I haven't been for years. I ought to go, really – it's probably a good place to pick up ideas.'

'And new friends,' said Kirsty Whittle, who was sitting close by.

Ackerman blushed but said nothing. She was a tall young woman, dark-haired, handsome, a militant feminist and Marxist who was a regular protest-goer and placard-carrier. I had the feeling that she could have told me more than she did about her notes and diagrams. Those scribbles seemed to me to be connected in some way to Amaryllis, which may sound a little paranoid, I know. Nobody's perfect.

While Ackerman and I were talking Ron Hastings came in on crutches with his left leg in a cast. His face looked as if somebody had stepped on it. 'What happened to you?' I said.

'Fell off a ladder.'

'When?'

'Late last night.'

'Around three in the morning?'

'Something like that.'

'Odd time to be up on a ladder.'

'Came home a little the worse for wear, found myself

locked out. Builders had left a ladder in the area. I went up it to my first-floor window, didn't quite get there. Do you want a note from my mother?'

'Sorry, I didn't mean to bug you.'

'Where were you at three o'clock this morning, Peter?'

'Glimming. Sleeping, rather.'

Did he look at me in a strange way? I wasn't sure.

'I hope your dreams were better than mine,' he said.

'You had bad ones last night?'

'Something muddled and unpleasant – can't remember.'

He sat down at his table and began to write in his sketchbook and I moved quietly away.

I made no further requests for glim images; everybody went back to whatever they'd been working on and I had very little to say for the rest of the day.

18

WALKING SPANISH

It was all I could do to restrain myself from looking for Amaryllis during the lunch break but I managed to hold back until I'd finished at the college. Where might she be – which of the places where we'd been together in our waking lives? And of course her availability was not unlimited: part of her time was taken up by the piano lessons she gave. I was pretty sure that she wanted to see me again but I recognised that she had to do it her way. Although she'd readily admitted being a weirdo there was always method in her madness: by not giving me a time and place to meet she was continually testing how tuned in I was to her.

As always, her face came to me half-turned-away. Probably she wouldn't want to be taken for granted after last night's glim. With that in mind I went to the first place where we'd seen each other in the unglim world: the Klein-bottle display in the Science Museum. There I waited as I'd done at the town library when I was fourteen and hoping for a glimpse of a girl I hadn't yet dared to speak to. I seemed to have a lot of breath in me and I had to keep exhaling.

In the flat unglim of this Thursday afternoon there was nobody else at the Klein-bottle display; I had it all to myself. Cindy Ackerman's reiterations came to mind, suggesting motion in the twists and turns of the glittering glass. As before, I turned my back on the bottles and felt their presence behind me. But then her written words, only half-remembered, came up in me like mental indigestion.

After a half-hour or so Amaryllis appeared, breathless. 'I couldn't get here any sooner,' she said. 'I have this woman in Wimbledon who insists on playing Scarlatti. She always loses but she always drags ten minutes more out of me.' She dropped her shoulder bag and flung herself into my arms. Not knowing when or even if I'd see her again, not even knowing her full name, I hugged her as if I could imprint myself on her by main force.

'You did it,' she said, 'you glimmed me to you,' and kissed me again.

'Do you remember what happened?' I said with my mouth against her neck.

'The bus and the Brass Hotel and Room 318? Yes, Peter, I remember all of it. I'm not alone any more.'

I was so touched that I almost started to cry. I kissed her again and again.

After a while I moved my face an inch or two away from hers and said, 'So I passed the test then, did I?'

'What do you mean, Peter?'

'It was my glim and I glimmed you into it.'

'Yes, you did, but it wasn't a test.'

'But it was important to you for me to bring you into *my* glim rather than be a guest in yours.'

'I wanted us to have a two-way connection, that's all,' she said, squirming a little away from the question.

This time her T-shirt said *WALKING SPANISH*. Did

she remember her T-shirt in last night's glim? I decided to let it be our unspoken thing. '*Walking Spanish?*' I said.

'It's from a Tom Waits song,' she said:

> *He rolled a blade up in his trick towel,*
> *They slap their hands against the wall.*
> *You never trip, you never stumble,*
> *He's walking Spanish down the hall.*

'I know the song very well,' I said. 'Are you walking Spanish down the hall?'

'I just like the sound of it; to me it always suggests going into the fourth dimension.'

'Spanish is the way to walk,' Lenore had said once. That was the past. But this moment with Amaryllis seemed to be a flash-ahead to a scene we hadn't yet got to, like the burning motorbike in *Easy Rider*. Her eyes had a somewhat foxy look and the expression on her face made me feel that the T-shirt was part of an in-joke that I was left out of. Somehow that fourth dimension got up my nose. 'Have you got a blade rolled up in your trick towel?' I said.

'No, Peter: no trick towel, no blade.' She was looking at me closely. 'All of a sudden you sound different. What is it?'

'Nothing. Do you ever trip and stumble?'

'Doesn't everyone?' She put her hand on my arm and brought her face within kissing range again. 'Are you going to tell me what's bothering you?'

'Who's bothered? Do you know Cindy Ackerman?'

'Royal College of Art?'

'That's the one.'

'She takes piano lessons from me. Why?'

I could feel an abyss opening under my feet so I jumped in. 'Ever see her outside of piano lessons?'

'Now and then. Where are you going with this?'

'Who knows? You said you'd gone out with Ron Hastings a few times. Did you sleep with him?'

'What kind of interrogation is this? Did I ever say I was a virgin? Whom I slept with before you is none of your goddam business.'

It was deep, that abyss, it was dark. It was full of miasmas and vapours that could damage my health. I inhaled deeply and continued to fall. 'It sure as hell is my business if we're going to be together from here on out. And it's certainly my business if other people are picking up glim vibes from us.'

She gave me a very strange look. 'What are you talking about?'

'Ron Hastings and Cindy Ackerman are both students of mine at the RCA. On Tuesday Hastings showed me Satan in yellow, orange, and pink pyjamas. Luminous ones. In last night's glim when we were on the bus I put my foot in his face and pushed him off the stairs. Today he showed up with his leg in a cast and his face full of bruises. And Cindy Ackerman came in with a page full of Klein-bottle action. Any idea where this could be coming from?'

The foxy look was gone; she looked scared, the way she'd been at the bus stop in the first glim. Her voice was her small not-wanting-to-be-alone voice. I remembered the feel of her nakedness, the scent of her skin. '*Are* we together from here on out?' she said very softly.

In the Science Museum the light was so different from the light of the brass lamps in Room 318! All around us were big glass boxes with cards that explained what was inside. 'I hope so,' I said. 'This isn't a good place to talk. Coffee?'

'Maybe a drink?' she said.

We headed for the Zetland Arms again. All the way there she clung to my arm and rubbed against me as much as possible. Well, I thought, I don't really like things to be too simple, do I.

Queenie and her master weren't there this time. There was the same quiet hubbub as before and the old clock from the Brewery, Reading, was still at its private midnight. I got our drinks and we sat there looking at each other. 'Please, Peter,' she said, 'talk to me.'

'You don't just tune in to people, do you,' I said. 'You make things happen. When I put my foot in Ron Hastings's face in the glim he fell off a ladder in the unglim.'

'*You* made that happen.'

'Because I was with you.'

She nodded and drank in silence for a while. Then she said, 'That's something I can't help; if I kick someone in a glim, they wake up with a bruise.'

'Or worse if you really get cross, I imagine.'

She shrugged. 'So don't make me cross.'

'I'll try not to. What was Hastings doing on that bus anyhow? Besides viewing your bottom?'

'As I said in the glim, no knickers and Hastings were *your* idea.'

'All right – I won't pester you about what he's been to you in the past, but is he anything to you now?'

'No, he isn't.'

'Because I don't need to know how many there've been before me but I need to know if it's just you and me now.'

'There's no one else now. I'm not even sure it *was* Hastings on the bus.'

'Who was it then?'

'I can't always explain everything, Peter. Is that all right?'

'I guess it'll have to be.' I reached for her hand. 'At least now when I touch you it's not a glim.'

'Not a glim,' she said. She was looking at our empty glasses.

I got us refills and when I sat down again it seemed to me there was a river between us and I couldn't see any stepping-stones. How real, I wondered, had last night been? 'Have you got a tattoo on your belly?' I said.

She nodded.

'Show me.'

She pulled up the bottom of her T-shirt, unzipped her jeans, and pulled down the waistband of her knickers to show me, in blue on her white skin, the yin-yang symbol.

'Let's go to my place,' I said.

'Please,' she said, 'not yet.'

'"Not yet"? But you've already been there.'

'Not in the way you're thinking of.'

'Jesus! We've already been naked together and as intimate physically as two people can be. What's the problem?'

'I'm bashful.'

'Bashful! That's not the Amaryllis I remember from the Brass Hotel.'

'Don't forget – that was your glim. Which reminds me, what about that T-shirt?'

'What T-shirt?'

'The one that said *Unnatural practices yes*. We didn't do anything that anyone could call unnatural. You glimmed the T-shirt, so tell me what it meant.'

'That's a private joke, sort of a codeword I'll explain to you another time. You've pointed out more than once that what happened at the Brass Hotel was my glim. Are you saying that you were only playing the part I gave you? You had nothing to do with what we did?'

'Of course I'm not saying that. Once the situation started going that way I wanted what happened as much as you did. But that was at the Brass Hotel. I'm not yet ready to do it at your place. Can you go along with that for a little while?'

'Sure, I'll take a cold shower when I get home. I know it was my glim rather than yours because you don't want to find yourself alone on that bus. You've said you don't know what's at Finsey-Obay but I think you do. What is it?'

She shook off the question and squeezed my hand, looking at me wistfully with her lips slightly parted. 'Peter, will you do something for me?'

'What?'

'I need you to glim something.'

'What, Amaryllis?'

She finished her whisky and looked at the empty glass. 'I have to be quiet for a moment before I tell you.'

I got up to go for refills. Between the glimworld and the unglim we were getting a fair amount of alcohol down our necks.

19

MEMORIES OF YEW

I go somewhere, I see something, and I don't always know what I saw until later. I know now, having consulted my tree books, that the tree that presided over the maze was a yew. Yews are either male or female and they live hundreds of years, maybe thousands. This was a male yew – you could tell by the tiny baby acorn-looking things on the leaf stalks – an old-man yew with many fissures in his trunk that was naked for ten feet or more before the crown of branches began. The trunk was tawny in the sunlight, took on reddish-purple tints when the sun went in. The crown had a sideways look, like a wizard's cloak blown by the wind. This was a lordly tree, a magisterial tree, clearly a tree of power.

'He doesn't like me,' said Lenore, 'Mr Old-Man Tree, but that's *his* problem.'

'First of all,' I said, 'how do you know it's a he, and second, how can you tell he doesn't like you?' I had no more idea of the tree's gender than I did of its kind.

'Don't be stupid,' she said. 'There are things one simply knows.'

Well, of course I could feel the communication between the old-man tree at the northern edge of the maze and the hollies at the southern edge which even I could identify because they had holly leaves. Hollies also have gender and I can't avoid the assumption that these were females of a certain age; they were not young groupie hollies.

Yews are commonly seen in churchyards, and my best tree book, published in 1842, says this is because sites of ancient Druidical worship were taken over by Christian churches. Evidently some of the Druids' best friends were yews even though every part of the tree is poisonous to humans and animals. The longbows of the English archers at Agincourt were yew – continental, it seems, not English; but yew they were, and the power of the heartwood and sapwood in them drove English arrows through French armour, knights, and horses at ranges of up to three hundred yards. It was Henry V's deployment of those yeoman archers that not only won the battle on that muddy field but made obsolete the idea of gentlemen's wars. So it's a serious tree, and Mr Old-Man Tree, though not in the arms trade, had in him the longbows of the spirit, and the effect on me was a serious one.

This was a turf maze, 57′ by 50′. You couldn't get lost in it because there were no hedges or walls and the whole thing was in plain sight as you walked it.

From a sketch by O.W. Godwin

The sign said:

> THIS TYPE OF TURF MAZE MAY DATE FROM MEDI-
> EVAL TIMES. SIMILAR MAZES ARE FOUND ELSE-
> WHERE IN ENGLAND AND IN CERTAIN FRENCH
> CATHEDRALS RELIGIOUS PENITENTS MAY HAVE
> FOLLOWED THE MAZE ON HANDS AND KNEES
> REPEATING PRAYERS.
>
> PLEASE RESPECT THIS MAZE.

We stood there looking at it while it looked back at us. It was screened from the road by dense hedges and it lived in a quiet all its own.

'Take off your shoes and socks,' said Lenore, removing hers.

'What for?'

'Because you don't want anything between your feet and it when we walk it.'

The turf paths were about a foot wide. Between them was something like sand-coloured aquarium gravel. This pattern of maze is called 'Troy Town'; in its simplest form it's known as a shepherd's maze and it turns up in culturally unconnected places from Scotland to Knossos. Seen from the holly trees as I looked towards the old-man tree the turf paths spread like ripples from the entry point.

This was only a week after our Beachy Head trip; the grass was cold and damp under our bare feet; Lenore's cheeks were rosy. She was wearing a long black skirt, black coat, a little black woollen hat with her long black hair streaming out from under it and a black scarf. At that moment the look on her rosy face framed by all that blackness made me think she might be ready to abandon the idea that I would make her unhappy.

'This maze is big stuff,' she said. 'Are you ready for it?'

'Ready for what exactly, Lenore?'

'Look at it. You might think you can simply follow a spiral to the centre but you can't. You start around it one way but then you double back and go the other way. You expect to get closer all the time but you keep passing through where you were before, passing through yourself as you inwind to the centre. And this isn't just a matter of walking around in a funny way; this is the earth we're walking on and it takes notice of our intention: if we do it together with the intention of inwinding ourselves to each other, then once we reach the centre that's it for ever. Do you want to do that?'

'Have you done this before?'

'No. I've never been here before and I've never done it with any other maze. It's just that I understand these things. So, do you want to do it?'

'Yes,' I said. I've mentioned before this that Lenore had a fateful bottom. Obviously there was more to her than that: her whole manner in whatever she said or did was fateful and hard to say no to.

So we did it. She walked ahead and I followed her naked feet as we went this way and that under a big and rapidly changing Willem van de Velde sky that lacked only a ship close-reefed in mountainous seas. I recalled the unfinished painting on Lenore's easel with its single figure. Why not both of us? As we walked we crossed and recrossed that beam of awareness between the old-man tree whose name I didn't know and the holly and each time I felt their response. I never asked Lenore if she felt it too, I kept that for myself. And she, of course, had things she kept to *her*self. No one tells another person everything.

Between the turf paths were dead leaves, almost black, rags and tatters of the year that was for ever gone. In that cloistered silence we moved alternately towards the centre and away from it, passing through the same curves in smaller and smaller circuits until we came to the centre and stood facing each other. 'For ever,' said Lenore, emphasising the two-wordness of it.

'For ever,' I said, meaning it but wondering who or what was actually saying it. Then we kissed in a for-ever kind of way.

'If we retrace our steps now we unwind what we inwound, don't we?' I said.

'We don't retrace our steps, we do it like this.' She stepped in a straight line from the centre to the outside of the maze and I followed.

'Walking Spanish?' I said.

'Walking straight,' she answered.

We put on our shoes and socks and looked back once before we left the maze which had already looked away from us. We must have been there longer than we thought; it was already dusk and the smell of the earth was strong. A distant crow said something and it came to us faintly in the twilight. A dog barked and there were lights in the windows of Troy Farm over the road.

Is it life that's so strange or is it just me? I was thinking, Well, that's the end of the beginning. And my mind said, Is it the beginning of the end?

'Are you sorry?' said Lenore.

'No,' I said, 'of course not.'

'Liar,' she said. 'That's all right. It was one of those things I had to do.'

We'd made this trip because she'd said she wanted to take me somewhere special but she wouldn't tell me where it was. For that reason I'd taken a camera with me and that's why I'm now able to know what we saw. Also, Lenore had broken off a bit of the needles of Mr Old-Man Tree which enabled me to make a positive identification. Obviously she wasn't worried about offending him. She had touched the tree; I hadn't. I'm the image-and-idea man but I hadn't touched that tree. Sometimes, looking at myself in the morning mirror or waking up in the middle of the night, I think about that.

Where the Ardley–Somerton road meets the B430 there's a Norman church with a gabled tower and a saddleback roof. It's made of Cotswold Stone and I think, having looked in my Pevsner *Oxfordshire Architectural Guide*, that it was St Mary's. Were there yews in the churchyard? I'm not sure. I go through life not always knowing what I see. Troy Farm, who own the maze we walked on, is also made of Cotswold Stone. Splendid buildings and outbuildings, undoubtedly passed from generation to generation. What must it be like to own an ancient maze?

On the trip out from London the M40 had been bleak, with only the van de Velde sky to provide interest above the articulated lorries and the onrush of miles. Going back the yellow lights provided a constant vanishing point, and into it we vanished.

But the maze and the walking of it didn't vanish. I had told Lenore that I was ready for it, that I wanted to do it, and afterwards I said I wasn't sorry I'd done it. But in the time that followed I often found myself shaking my head and saying, aloud to myself if I was alone, 'Why did I do that?'

20

THE DARK ROAD

When I returned to the table (lurching a little, I noticed) Amaryllis wasn't there and I thought, Well that's it for today. When am I going to see her again? In my glims? Then she came back and I exhaled.

'I had to pee,' she said. 'Did you think I'd gone?'

'I was pretty sure you wouldn't leave me to drink all this alone,' I said. I hadn't noticed that the sounds around us had stopped but now I noticed them coming back with the lights both plain and coloured, the figures moving and still, the music and the voices and the smoke. Had that happened before? We both sat down, lifted our whiskies to our mouths, drank, put the glasses down, and looked at each other. 'You were saying,' I said.

'What?'

'You were going to tell me something you needed me to glim.'

'Yes.' She gulped down some beer, rubbed her face, ran her hand over her hair. 'It's hard because I get mixed up between my glim life and the unglim and I think some of my memories are false. But even a false memory is all right if it makes you feel good and doesn't hurt anyone, don't you think?'

'I suppose so.'

'So much of life is like driving on a dark road and you can't see what's beyond the headlamps' beams.'

'If you keep moving ahead,' I said, 'you get to see what was in the dark a while back.'

'Could you glim for me . . . ?'

'Yes, Amaryllis, what?'

'Could you glim for me a dark road in America?'

'Where in America is this road?'

'I'm not sure. Maybe Maine, maybe Massachusetts. Have you been to those places?'

'Yes, I have.'

'This is a very lonesome road in the middle of nowhere. I remember piney woods on both sides.'

I saw a yew tree, heard the District Line rails cry, *Wheats-yew!* Saw the oncoming train circling, returning.

'What?' she said.

'Sorry, you said "piney woods".'

'That's how they say it in that part of the country, I think. Piney woods on both sides. And a little white petrol station with a red roof and a little red cupola. There's a small sign with a winged red horse on it. *MOBILGAS*, it says on the sign which is hanging from a bracket on a tall pole with a lamp on it. Three red petrol pumps with lit-up white globes on top, also with the winged red horse. It's evening, a summer evening with the sky still light. The lamp over the sign lights up the boughs of the nearest pines. I remember the stillness of that summer evening, the lonesomeness of that empty road – it was such a long time between cars. There was a man standing by one of the pumps and he made it all even more lonesome. He was wearing a waistcoat and a tie. White shirt.' She began to cry.

'Amaryllis, why are you crying?'

'The look of those lit-up globes on the pumps and the lamp over the sign and the sky that's still light . . .'

'Amaryllis, what you've described is a painting by Edward Hopper. It's called *Gas*.'

'Well, I can't help it if he painted a picture of that road and that petrol station – I was there on holiday with my parents when I was five or six or seven and I can see it in my mind.'

'OK, I'll try to glim an Edward Hopper. Is there anything down that road beyond the limits of the picture?'

'Why do you keep calling it a picture?'

'I can't help it – it *is* a picture, a very well-known one that you must have seen a reproduction of and made into a false memory. How old are you?'

'Twenty-eight.'

'This is 1999. So you were born in 1971. Say you were seven when you were in Maine or Massachusetts, that brings us up to 1978. By then I doubt that you could find petrol pumps like that in America. Maybe not even in Tibet. Surely you've seen reproductions of Hopper paintings?'

'I don't remember,' she said rather sullenly.

'It's hard for me to believe that someone who plays Chopin hasn't also become aware of Edward Hopper.'

'What are you,' she said, 'some kind of snulture cob? Culture. Snob.'

'I guess I am, now that you mention it. Anyhow, what's down that road? If anything.'

'One thing at a time, OK? Let's just put me on that road and we'll go on from there.'

'If it's my glim we could well end up in the bushes.'

'Is that what I am to you? Your glim totty?'

'You're many things to me; that's just one of them. Goodness knows I've made unglim advances but you don't seem to want to be my unglim totty.'

'I thought you were different.'

'Different from what? I'm different from a horse or a crocodile but I might well be similar in some respects to other men.'

'Don't speak to me about respect,' she said in a very dignified way. 'The question is, are you going to glim that road for me or not?'

'Of course I'll do it. I can't help wondering, though, Amaryllis, why you don't glim it yourself. Your recall is so visid, so visually ibid. Vivid. So why don't you?'

'You have to keep asking questions, don't you. How many times do I have to tell you that if I do the glim it'll be that bus stop again and I'd rather it weren't. OK? Do you have a prolbem with that?'

'No prolbem, sweetheart. Your whim is my engraved-in-brass. Or chiselled-in-stone, as the case may be.'

'Right. That's it, then. See you in your glim if you can be bothered to make the effort.'

'My place again, right?'

'I think you can prolly go it alone this time. Let's just a greena bedtime, OK?'

'Did you say greena bedtime?'

'You neenry peat everything. Two o'clock all right? That's 02:00.'

'Righty-o. Let me see you home. You may be just ever so slightly tired and emotional.'

'You're very kind,' she said tearfully. 'I know you're a true friend. But if you could find me a cab I'd rather. Please forgive me, I know I'm a lot of trouble.'

'You? Trouble? Never!' We kissed and hugged and after a while I found her a cab and put her into it. I didn't hear what address she gave the driver. And I still didn't know her last name.

21

BIRD-WOMEN

'One cannot be sure,' wrote art critic Lytton Toomey in the *Guardian*, 'whether Peter Diggs's bird-women are sirens or harpies. They are by turns seductive, housewifely, terrifying, comical, and disgusting. Certainly they sing, as evidenced in the rowdy pub scenes where they appear, as everywhere else, topless. When partying they flaunt other parts as well. Shopping in the supermarket, their demeanour, despite the partial nudity, is modest. In other situations their talons are frightening, their habits unclean. The *mise-en-scène* of the pictures is to some extent Hammer Gothic but the style, the atmospherics and the general look call to mind the Symbolists, particularly Redon and Khnopff.'

Toomey was reviewing my 1994 show at the Fanshawe Gallery which had a rather good press and was, surprisingly for me, a sellout: in earlier shows I'd never sold more than two or three paintings. When I find a theme I can do something with I tend to stay with it for a while; I'd done that with *Don Quixote* and I'd done it with *Orlando Furioso*. If I'd painted six versions of Angelica being rescued from the sea monster by Ruggiero

I think I could have sold them all; I hadn't realised at the time the commercial possibilities of bondage and bestiality.

Lenore had her own opinion of my bird-women. 'For Christ's sake,' she said, 'if you're afraid of women why don't you just come out as a queer instead of pissing about with harpies?'

'Any sensible man is afraid of women,' I said. 'You're just jealous because you haven't got a gallery and you probably never will because all you do is your notebooks and paintings you don't finish.'

'The difference between us, you poor schmuck, is that I'm concerned with seeing and you're concerned with selling. And you've well and truly sold out with your birds with tits and women's heads.'

'No, I haven't. I've been exploring a theme that's worth exploring while you've been hugging your images to yourself because you're afraid of submitting a finished work to judgement. You're afraid that you'll be told you're not as good as you need to be. Whatever happened, by the way, to that painting of the figure on the maze?'

'I never intended to finish that one, stupid; that guy is still walking.'

'And you're still talking, but only to yourself.'

'Right. The next sound you hear will be your front door slamming as I leave you to your harpies.'

'For ever?'

No answer but the front door slamming.

That wasn't the end; she rang me up the next day and I took her out to dinner at the Blue Elephant. The foliage, the gentle plashing of the fountain and the rain-forest humidity had a calming effect on both of us. What we had between us was always ready to erupt like a dormant volcano; there was only a little bit of lava running down the mountain that time but it was definitely not the safest picnic spot.

22

THE ESSENTIAL AMARYLLIS

I wanted Amaryllis to be with me but she wasn't. I went up to the studio and looked at the warm-toned empty canvas. I went through my sketches, trying to find her essential self in them. Seeing her in the glimworld and the unglim both was confusing; I trusted my senses, I wasn't hallucinating her, yet almost she seemed a creature of my imagination. With her unpredictable comings and goings she lacked the solid reality of persons who were where you expected to find them when you expected to find them.

Until now I'd thought only of what *I* wanted; I'd never considered what she might want other than not to be alone. Maybe she didn't want me at all; maybe I was only a means to some end I knew nothing of. And was I perhaps using her in some way I didn't know about?

The light was waning; I turned on the colour-corrected fluorescents and began to develop her face in cool tones. I remembered how she'd looked in the first glim, *her* glim in which she was thin and haggard. In spite of her confidence, even arrogance sometimes, I sensed that the thin woman with the straw-coloured hair was still how she thought of herself – unsure, afraid, searching for something she'd never found, and that face wanted to show through the winsome beauty of the Pre-Raphaelite nymph.

The painting was going the way yesterday's drawing had: it was better than I was ordinarily capable of doing. In the face that was coming to life on the canvas was the going to the cliff's edge, the clear-eyed weirdness under the misty beauty. In searching for Amaryllis I lost myself, and by the time I stopped and cleaned my palette and brushes I didn't know where she left off and I began. 'The idea is in the image.' How many times had I said that? And when I said it, was I just talking bollocks? Amaryllis's image was by now indelibly imprinted on me but what was the idea of her? She was a fair one who constantly beckoned, but to what? For that matter, what was the idea of me? Did I even want to know?

How quickly the strange becomes the usual! I was in love with a woman who was most responsive to me when we were both asleep. Between the glim and the unglim, where was reality? I went out on the balcony and looked to the west. There was the moon, one night past the full, sailing serenely in and out of cloud-wrack. Perhaps Amaryllis too was looking at it now. It was 01:35.

23

TO MAINE OR MASSACHUSETTS

I did the Möbius, watching the slider go around the twist again and again while I saw in my mind Amaryllis's delicate sweet belly and her yin-yang tattoo. Soon my head went wide, then long, but it was easier this time, with no nausea.

When the glim came I was standing by the Edward Hopper Mobilgas station looking down that lonesome road in the summer evening in a silence made up of the chirping of crickets. The air was very fresh and it was quite cool. The Mobilgas sign creaked a little as it swung in the breeze. There were bats flitting against a purple not-yet-dark sky. I threw a pebble into the air and one of them followed it down as it fell to the ground. Loneliness, I thought, is the essential human condition. Everything else is gravy.

The man by the pumps was putting cans of oil in a rack. 'Looks like a slow evening here,' I said.

'They're all slow,' he said. 'And for my sins I had to get stuck here.'

'You sound English.'

'Look, mate, it's your glim. When you learn to talk Maine or Massachusetts I'll do the same, OK?'

'Listen, buddy, I'm as American as you are.'

'I doubt it. Where you from?'

'Born in Pennsylvania.'

'Where you from now?'

'London.'

'London, England?'

'Yes.'

'Shit.'

'Why'd you say that?'

'My daughter went to London with a tour group. They went to a museum and there was an unmade bed: dirty sheets all rumpled and a used tampon and a used condom. In a museum! They call that art over there, do they?'

'Try not to think about it,' I said. 'Think Edward Hopper.'

'He's the only reason I keep this miserable place going. Nobody ever stops here.'

I shook my head sympathetically. 'Gets pretty cool here in the evenings, doesn't it.'

'No use breaking my balsam about it. Turn up the heat if you're cold.' He finished what he was doing and disappeared.

There was a pale glimmer down the road: Amaryllis's T-shirt. As she drew closer I saw that the words on it were:

The world is whatever is the case.

'Is that Wittgenstein?' I said.

'Don't ask me, it's your glim, Mr Snulture.' She kissed me thoroughly, then took my hand and shoved it inside her jeans and knickers. 'Everything north and south of my tattoo is yours,' she breathed in my ear. 'Also east and west, front and back included. Because you're my kind of glimmer. And you're reliable.'

'I'm not putting words in your mouth, am I? Since it's my glim, I mean.'

'Stop worrying and kiss me.'

I did.

'When it's your glim I feel a lot freer,' she said, putting her hand inside my shirt.

'I'm not complaining.'

'Let's just walk for a while. Smell the pines!'

'Just as I yewsed to.'

'What?'

'Nothing. I mumble sometimes.'

We held hands and walked down the road as the sky grew darker. The crickets carried on cricketing; a bird said something; somewhere an owl hooted. There were no cars; that dark road had only the particularity of the pines and the crickets and the owl and the other bird, the evening breeze and nothing more – none of my daily concerns and worries. Except perhaps one or two.

'I remember this road from when I was little,' said Amaryllis. 'I can feel myself passing through myself to that time when everything around me was so much bigger and the time in front of me had no end to it. Do you feel realer in this glim than you do when you're awake?'

'Maybe I do.'

'You don't like this road. I can tell.'

'It's all right; I don't mind it.'

'Do you like just walking with me, not doing anything more than this?'

'I like walking with you, talking with you, anything with

you, Amaryllis.' Being with her was so weird that I felt completely at home with it.

She kissed me and we paused for a little quiet snogging. A few minutes later as we came around a bend we saw the Pines Motel with its green neon sign that said VACANCY. 'On the other hand,' said Amaryllis, 'why fight it?'

The place looked fairly run-down but all we actually needed was a bed so I opened the screen door of the office and we went in. There was a long strip of flypaper hanging from the ceiling, well furnished with flies. There was a portrait of Cotton Mather on the wall below a sampler that said JESUS LOVES YOU. There was a calendar from Smallville Hardware & Building Supplies Est. 1929. The picture on the calendar was *Gas* by Edward Hopper.

The owner was an American-Gothic sort of woman with silvery hair pulled back in a bun, steel-rimmed spectacles, a faded print dress, a jet brooch, and a strong smell of camphor. She was reading a large much-used family Bible that weighed about three kilos, the kind with tooled leather covers and a brass clasp. She marked her place with the ribbon, gave us her beady attention, and said in a starchy voice, '*Psalm 137*: "By the rivers of Babylon, there we sat down, yea, we wept, when we remembered Zion."'

Amaryllis burst into tears. 'Oh, Peter darling,' she murmured brokenly with her face against my neck, 'I *do* remember Zion! No one has ever glimmed me the way you do.'

That was the first time she'd said anything about old glimmers. I'd never expected her to be without sexual experience but thinking about her being pulled into someone else's glims made me wonder if I was on a road to nowhere with her. I held her close and stroked her hair and didn't say anything.

'Please stop that long enough to check in,' said Mrs Gothic. 'What you get up to or down to in your room is none of my business. Checkout time is at noon.'

We checked in as Mr and Mrs Peter Diggs. I paid in advance with American money that I found in my pocket and Mrs Gothic gave me a key to one of the small cabins that stood in a row with the paint flaking off their clapboard sides. There were a Coke machine and an ice machine but no other visible amenities. I was confident that the mattress would be damp.

The room lived up to expectations. It smelled musty. There was no telephone or TV. There was a bare bulb in the ceiling which gave a pale-yellow tint to the darkness. There was one shaky bedside lamp with a 40-watt bulb. I lifted the chenille bedspread and bedclothes and felt the mattress: damp. Amaryllis sat down on the bed, looking not altogether in the mood for love.

I was expecting another religious slogan on the wall but I was surprised to see a reproduction of Ryder's *Moonlight*. Well of course it was my glim, wasn't it. Had there been a moon when we were on the dark road? I didn't think so.

For a while I stood in front of the picture studying the little pitching vessel and the obscure figure huddled by the mast. The storm had passed but the loose sail streamed forward, untended, while the hull drove before the wind under a full moon. Was there someone at the tiller? Hard to tell. If there wasn't, or if the rudder had gone, what was keeping the boat from broaching to? Two little dark clouds, like lost and wandering souls, moved across the clean-washed moonlit sky. That man huddled by the mast, would he ever get home?

'I *do* know Hopper's work,' said Amaryllis, 'and Ryder's too. I studied at the RCA but I left the year before you arrived. That's where I met Ron Hastings and Cindy Ackerman.'

'There's always something new about you, isn't there,' I said.

'About you too. What kind of a dump did you glim us into? Are you trying to tell me something or what?'

'I can only get the glim started, you know that. I didn't do the Brass Hotel and its decor and I didn't do most of this. I could certainly do with a drink about now.'

'Me too, but you seem to have left out the mini-bar when you glimmed this room.'

'We didn't pass an off-licence on our way here. Maybe they haven't got any in greater Smallville. Maybe there's still prohibition out here.'

'They call them liquor stores in America,' said Amaryllis. 'Maybe you should have glimmed us closer to town.'

'Well, I was following your instructions, wasn't I. You asked for the Edward Hopper Mobilgas station and I didn't bother to glim beyond that. Maybe one of your old glimmers could have done better.'

She looked at me reproachfully, more in sorrow than in anger. 'It's very mean-spirited of you to throw that up to me. I've been open with you and this is what I get for it. You haven't told me anything about your past but if you haven't glimmed others before me I'm sure it's only because you didn't know how to.'

'Amaryllis,' I said, 'mightn't life be simpler if we just did things in the ordinary way and slept in the same bed at night and glimmed our individual glims the same as everyone else? Please don't start crying.' Because she looked as if she was ready to.

'Goddam it, Peter, how many times do I have to tell you

that if I glim alone I'll find myself on that lousy bus again and I'd rather not, OK?'

'All right, but do you mind telling me why we're out here in the boondocks?'

She got up and came to me and leant against me tiredly and I could feel how much she needed me. 'I wanted to be here with you,' she said in her smallest voice, 'and I thought you wanted to be here with me.'

'I *do*,' I said with my arms around her. 'Was it just the dark road you wanted us to come to or does the road lead to something else?'

Still in her smallest voice she said, 'I weep when I remember Zion. Are you going to let the phone keep ringing?'

'There's no phone here,' I said. 'It's the postman.' I woke up and answered the door and he gave me *Nosferatu* and *The Creature from the Black Lagoon* that I'd ordered from Amazon.com.

24

THE BORGO PASS

The voice of Mona Spägele, spidering delicately in a dim silken web of lamentation, rose and fell while the rain drummed on the studio windows. Barbara Strozzi had written *L'Eraclito Amoroso* in seventeenth-century Venice, tracing note by note the shadowy shapes of love's sorrow for soprano, viola da gamba, bass lute, harpsichord, and raindrops. Barbara Strozzi with no CD player, no electricity, working perhaps by candlelight, perhaps by rainlight.

What the painting needed, I saw now, was more space, more background: mountains, moonlight, mists rising where eyes gleamed in the darkness. The 18 x 24″ canvas was too small. I put it aside, stretched a 24 x 32″ canvas, toned it with cadmium red and alizarin crimson, and started again with Amaryllis's face somewhat larger than before, ghosting it in as lightly as I could. Dark brooding mountains, yes, against a purply-pale sky with a full moon cold and implacable. A great ruined castle high on the peak. The Borgo Pass in Transylvania came to life under my brush, the dim road wending its midnight way through the Carpathians to the castle.

By now her face came easily to me but the image refused

to yield the idea of her. I'd been seeing her from the outside and I hadn't really got past the Pre-Raphaelite nymph of her which was well enough in its way but by no means the whole story; there was another face under that one, a stronger, darker face. There were things to be done around the mouth, more work needed on the eyes, subtle emphases to be made here and there to bring out the inner reality of this woman who was not simply to be taken in at a glance.

Wisely or not, I was in love with her but I was tired of dividing my life between the glimworld and the unglim, I wanted to be with her in the ordinary way, with surnames, telephone numbers, addresses, and meeting times and places in the waking world. I had begun to wonder about my own part in our glims and I'd become suspicious of my arrangements at the Pines Motel with its damp mattress and its 40-watt bulbs. I wanted to see Amaryllis but today some little edge of resentment kept me from hurrying from place to place trying to find her.

The rain was steady; it was a drowsy kind of day and I slipped into something like a trance; my hand was working autonomously while my mind was between sleeping and waking. By mid-afternoon I'd had enough for a while and lay down on the studio couch for a nap. I didn't want to glim Amaryllis – all I wanted was the sort of kip I'd been able to enjoy before I met her. In a very short time, however, I found myself in the Carpathian Mountains, at the Borgo Pass. Dark clouds raced across the face of the full moon and the howling of wolves came to me on the wind.

I was turning this way and that, fearful of an attack from behind, when I heard the sound of hooves and the clatter of wheels. Four splendid coal-black horses came into view drawing a *calèche*. Amaryllis was on the driver's seat, cloaked and booted and wearing a broad-brimmed hat. 'Get in!' she shouted as she reined in the horses.

I climbed in. The top was down, the wind was rising. Amaryllis's hair streamed out from under her hat. 'Where are we going?' I said.

'Back to the Pines Motel.' Her words were almost carried away by the wind. She shook the reins, whooped to the horses, and off we went, jolting along the road out of the mountains and the wind and the howling of wolves, down through a valley where the mists were rising, and on to the dark road through the pines, the crickets and the hooting of the owl to the Edward Hopper Mobilgas station. The moon by then had set. The man in the white shirt was stocking the rack with cans of motor oil again when we pulled into the forecourt.

Amaryllis threw him the reins as she climbed down and he unharnessed the horses and led them away. She was once more in jeans and T-shirt as we left the station. The T-shirt said:

Never play cards with a man called Doc. Never eat at a place called Mom's. Never sleep with a woman whose troubles are worse than your own.

Nelson Algren, *A Walk on the Wild Side*

Amaryllis took the front of the T-shirt between thumb and forefinger, pulled it away from her body, and looked down at it. 'This is what I mean,' she said as if answering a question I hadn't been aware of asking.

'What about it?'

'I've never read Nelson Algren.'

113

'So?'

'You glimmed this shirt and put me into it.'

'I never said I didn't.'

We walked in silence for a while, listening to the crickets. 'Well, I'm a little confused,' she said, 'about the way these glims are going.'

'I'm listening.'

We were at the Pines Motel by then. We went to our cabin and she took the key out of her pocket and unlocked the door. 'Honey, I'm home,' she said, and tilted her head to one side and looked at me questioningly.

'What?' I said.

'Mildew Haven,' she said. 'Our little love nest.'

I didn't say anything.

'When we got here I was feeling good about you,' she continued, 'but if you were feeling good about me I wonder why you glimmed me into this no-star establishment. Is it that you don't really like me? You have doubts about this whole thing? What?'

'I love you, Amaryllis. I've told you that waking and I've told you that glimming and it's true. But I'm confused too – this motel came from somewhere in my mind that I wasn't intending to go into. I don't fully understand what's happening with us.'

'I wanted to be here with you,' she said, 'because there's a place farther down this road that I wanted to go to with you but I wasn't quite ready for it yet. Do you know what that place is?'

I saw black velvet, silver writing. 'I'm not sure,' I said.

'I think you are and I don't quite know where we go from here.' There were scattered drops of rain at the windows, then the drops came closer together until they were a steady drumming downpour. The roof leaked in several places. I put the wastebasket under the worst one; the others had to do without. Fortunately the bed wasn't under any of them. 'At least we're out of the rain,' she said, 'mostly.'

'I'm sorry about this motel, Amaryllis. I'm kind of mixed up but I do love you.'

'In that case,' she said as she opened her arms to me, 'maybe our body heat will dry out the mattress.'

It did, or at least it made us forget the dampness. Later as we lay there pleasantly entangled Amaryllis said, 'This next place that I want to go to – I have a feeling that you know it and you *don't* want to go there. Am I right?'

'I'll tell you what I think the problem is,' I said as the doorbell rang.

'You'd better answer the door,' she said.

'This cabin has no doorbell,' I said.

'All the more reason to answer it. Maybe it's something really urgent.'

'Like what?'

'Like me wanting to come in out of the rain.'

'Oh,' I said, 'well, then.' And I woke up and went down to the front door to let her in.

25

BOWL OF CHERRIES

She was wearing a yellow mac with streams of water running down it and a sopping wet broad-brimmed green canvas hat. Her plimsolls were soaked and a puddle was forming around her as we kissed on the doorstep. 'Were you with me just now at the Pines Motel?' I asked.

'Have you forgotten so soon?' she said with a lewd grin, making more puddles as I drew her inside.

'Never, but if you were with me in the glim you must have been asleep.'

'That's right; I fell asleep on the train from Embankment.'

'But the doorbell just now woke me out of the Pines Motel where you told me to answer the door, and at that moment you must have been walking here from Fulham Broadway.'

'But glims do that: you heard the doorbell and the glim backed up to give you what led up to that sound.'

'Funny how the mind does that.'

'The mind's the funniest place there is.'

'Isn't it though. I hadn't expected the Pines Motel and you, I was only wanting a little kip – I hadn't been trying to pull you.'

'Maybe you were and didn't know it. Anyhow, I hope you didn't mind being interfered with.'

I kissed her. 'I closed my eyes and thought of England.'

'Plucky little man. I've come all the way from Maine or Massachusetts and I'm about ready for a drink.'

'Boilermakers as usual?'

'What's a boilermaker?'

'Whisky with a beer chaser.'

'I don't want to chase it too far.'

'No problem – in this house the bitter comes in less-than-pints.'

Amaryllis hung up her wet things and followed me into the kitchen where I got two cans of John Smith and glasses and a tray. Then we went up to the living-room where the whisky was. I poured us two large Glenfiddichs and we clinked glasses. 'Here's looking at you, kid,' I said.

'Here's looking right back.' The whisky went down beautifully, the bitter rounded it off but I felt a slight edge in the air. Her T-shirt said:

> *Life is just*
> *a bowl of cherries.*
> *Don't be so serious –*
> *life's too mysterious.*
>
> Lew Brown &
> Ray Henderson

'It's nice that you give the credit,' I said.

'Where it's due I always do.'

'How do you choose your T-shirt for the day?'

'I have three T-shirt drawers: Random; Support; and Think.'

'What's in Think?'

'They're mostly blank.'

'Which drawer is this one from?'

'Random. That's the one with the most shirts in it.'

'Is that the drawer you picked me out of when you tuned in that afternoon in South Ken tube station?'

'You weren't random; you were putting out Find-me vibes. So I found you.'

'Did you think I was lost?'

'Maybe *you* did.'

'But today I'm not lost. Are you?'

'No more than usual.' We drank to that and chased it not too far. The rain on the windows curtained us off from the world.

'Speaking of T-shirts, Peter – what about the ones I wear in your glims, what drawers do they come from?'

'The same drawers where the Brass Hotel and the Pines Motel live.'

'Very big, very deep?'

'Deeper than some, I guess; shallower than others.'

'Do you remember the words on the T-shirt I took off at the Brass Hotel?'

'Yes, I remember them very well.'

'Back then you said that *Unnatural practices yes* was a sort of code. What do those words mean to you?'

I was in love with Amaryllis but we hadn't yet reached a point where we told each other everything – in her case, not even a surname. Pondering what to say I went back in my memory to a time that was blurred and out-of-focus but big and vivid on the screen of my mind.

26

UNNATURAL PRACTICES

I might have been four or five, I'm not sure which, and we were either in Maine or Massachusetts. Afterwards I could never get Uncle Stanley and Aunt Florence to talk about it. We were on holiday in our car. At the start of each day's drive Mum sat up front with Dad and I sat in the back with Stanley and Florence, between Stanley and the door. I kept getting carsick; it was an old Chevrolet and the smells of petrol and upholstery and Stanley's cigars and aftershave combined with the motion of the car invariably brought me to a point where we'd have to stop so I could get out and throw up. After that they'd put me in the front seat and Mum would move to the back. I was less likely to become nauseated in the front but they never let me sit there until after I'd vomited; they clung to the theory that I could pull myself together and not be carsick.

I remember a red sunset all desolate like the end of the world. On the radio a woman was singing 'There Is a Balm in Gilead'. There was a dark road through pine woods. There was a shop that sold souvenirs. There was a jar of horehound drops. Dad bought me some. There was a black-velvet pillow with silver script lettering on it: *For you I pine, for you I balsam.*

It smelled all piney, that pillow, like the dark woods of eternal rest in Jesus. The silver paint had its own smell. There was a black cat that purred and rubbed against my legs. It looked up at me with its big green eyes as if it would speak but it didn't. 'She wants to be remembered,' said the old woman who ran the shop. 'Her name is Josephine; she has dreams.' She was dressed all in black, that old woman. I wished I could have had that piney pillow but we never went back there.

That evening Mum and Dad had a terrible row; they were shouting at each other and flinging their arms about but I couldn't make out what they were saying. All I remember is Mum crying and Dad saying, 'After all these years!' Then they left me at the motel with Stanley and Florence while they went out. I think we watched *I Love Lucy*. Mum and Dad never came back; they were killed in a car crash. Stanley said, 'Death is always there like a street on a Monopoly board; you could land on it at any time with no warning.' I remember that but not the place where he said it.

That same night I was put to bed in Stanley and Florence's room. I was too little to know then but I think now they must have been drinking because they behaved as if I wasn't there. I pretended to be asleep while they took their clothes off and got ready for bed and that was the first time I saw a woman naked. When they were in bed Stanley said to Florence, 'You want unnatural practices? I'll *give* you unnatural practices.' I wasn't sure what they were doing but Florence kept saying no and she cried afterwards.

The funeral took place back home. The caskets were closed and there were lilies and the smell of them. A woman I didn't know sang 'There Is a Balm in Gilead' and I felt as if that song and the desolate red sunset had followed me from the dark road and the pine woods. Writing this now I have the sudden crazy notion that everybody at birth is issued a little box of images, music, words and a few other things that will appear and reappear in varying combinations all through life.

Stanley and Florence had no children, and after the funeral I lived with them in Connecticut until they sent me off to boarding school. Florence was always kind to me. Stanley had bad breath and the whole house stank from his cigars. I was very curious about unnatural practices and tried to find out more about them by peeping through the keyhole of their bedroom whenever possible. Stanley caught me at it and used his belt on me, which made me more cautious but did not deter me in my researches.

Whatever I was able to observe seemed pretty unnatural to me, but schoolfellows more sophisticated than I explained that what Stanley and Florence did was the usual thing done by men and women. What I'd seen and heard through the keyhole, the grunting and the outcries and the heavy work of it, fascinated me, and I looked forward to a time when the world of the keyhole would open to me.

What I wrote a few moments ago about a little box of images, music, words and so on – I know what put that into my mind: it was the memory of Stanley's cigar boxes. He stored screws, nuts and bolts and other bits of ironmongery in the empty ones and I had several as well in which I kept marbles and string and various treasures of the moment.

There must be cigar boxes all over the world with bits of people's lives in them – photographs and postcards from everywhere, letters in all languages in cigar boxes in Mongolian yurts, bedouin tents in the Sahara, Indian huts on the Amazon. I think Stanley smoked La Coronas but that might be a false memory. The scene on the lid that I recall is probably a conflation of several: a gorgeous world of pyramids and palm trees, distant blue skies, balloon ascensions, racing locomotives, fallen pillars, and wheels of commerce and industry presided over by the beautiful goddess of the cigar-box lid. In my more fanciful moments I wonder if cigar boxes glim, and if the scene on the lid is what they're glimming.

I have no cigar boxes now, but they live somewhere in my memory, and as I call up one from my years with Stanley and Florence I open it and see, at the top of the several layers of this time-capsule, a broken mother-of-pearl penknife, a postcard from Crystal Cave, a roll of caps from a toy pistol, some Indian-head pennies and a silver dollar, two aggies and a glass shooter, a souvenir ballpoint pen in which a tiny Kong climbs the Empire State Building, a coil of the strong-smelling string called tarred ganja, and a school photograph of Clara Wilson.

The little black-and-white photograph of Clara, taken when we were both nine, has almost nothing of the real nine-year-old Clara I remember in an empty hayloft in the old barn where the dust-motes danced in the sunlight that came through the cracks in the siding. It was summer, the air was warm and lazy with the drone of cicadas. I see her now with her clear blue eyes, her little smile, and the sunlight backlighting her fair hair. She was from Milwaukee and she was visiting next door. She brought with her distance and enchantment and I can't remember how, or if, I led up to it but I asked her if she would show me hers if I'd show her mine and she said yes. It's still there in my mental cigar box, her very gracious yes.

27

THE BECKONING OTHER

'Have you fallen asleep?' said Amaryllis.

'What?'

'I asked you what the words *Unnatural practices yes* meant to you and you seemed to go into a trance. Are you all right?'

'I'm fine. It was just something from my childhood; I used to think that anything men and women did in bed was an unnatural practice because of something my uncle said one time.'

'Childhoods,' she said. 'Everybody has one.' She leaned back and crossed her arms on her chest. 'I like the rain; maybe we don't need to talk, maybe we could just drink and be together and listen to the rain.'

'Whatever you say, Amaryllis.' So we did that: she arranged herself on the couch with her bare feet tucked under her and I took the chair and footstool opposite. We drank and listened to the rain while I mentally undressed her. I thought of us wide-awake and naked in front of the fire but it was too warm for a fire. Our glasses were empty; I refilled them.

'The rain is putting me to sleep,' she said. 'How about some music?'

'Sure, but let's go up to the studio. I want to see you and the painting together.'

'Have you finished it already?'

'No, it's still developing but I want to see how it looks to me when you're standing next to it.'

The rainlight was wonderful in the studio; the rain on the windows was like the muffled drums of time. I removed the Barbara Strozzi disc from the CD player and put in *The Art of Fugue*, the recording by Musica Antiqua Köln – it seemed right for this particular afternoon. It's more painterly than the keyboard versions; the colours of the instrumental voices, like the Invisible Man's bandages, help to reveal what can't be seen directly.

As the voices went over and under, advancing and retreating and passing through themselves, Amaryllis put down her drink and put her hands over her ears. 'Please stop that awful Klein-bottle music,' she said, 'before I throw up.'

'Sorry!' I said. I removed the Bach and inserted the Barbara Strozzi which was of course much better music for viewing the painting. Why had I put on the other?

'Yes,' said Amaryllis as Mona Spägele's voice mingled with the rainlight. 'That's more like it.'

When I replaced Bach on the shelf the painting was not in my field of vision and I wasn't watching Amaryllis as she took up a position in front of the canvas but I heard the silence that followed. When I turned I saw only the back of the easel but I saw Amaryllis's face and she had gone deathly pale.

'Amaryllis,' I said. 'What is it?'

She rushed past me and I followed her to the bathroom and held her hair out of the way while she vomited into the toilet. When she'd finished she went to the sink and rinsed her mouth and face.

'Are you all right?' I said.

'Fine. Too many boilermakers, need a little fresh air.'

'It's still raining.'

'Fine. Rain's good. Fresh.' She went downstairs fast but wobbly, put on her things, slung her shoulder bag, saw me putting on my mac, said, 'No taxi, need to walk. By self. Don't come with,' and lurched off into the wet.

I went back to the studio, went around the easel to stand in front of the painting. The misty moonlight was gone. There were no Carpathians, no Borgo Pass, no ruined castle. No Amaryllis. Broad daylight, and there was Lenore, all in black, her face pale, her long black hair whipping in the wind. She was standing at the edge of the cliff with the sea behind her. Her right arm was raised as she beckoned me to follow. Was she shaping 'Yes!' with her mouth? My hearing, doing its new thing, seemed to shut down so that for a moment the music and the sound of the rain were gone. Then they came back, and with them the silence that Amaryllis left behind her.

28

WHAT NOW?

Was I awake or was I glimming? With my right hand I pinched my left arm and it felt solid and real but then every part of me always felt real in glims. I picked up the telephone and dialled 123. 'At the sound of the third stroke it will be six-thirteen and thirty seconds,' said a cultured female voice. Pip pip pip. I put down the phone. The woman had spoken in the weary cut-glass tones of someone who really had no time for me. What had happened to the Accurist man who always gave Accurist time in such a strong and manly way? You knew where you were with him; his voice was like a tall building with all the lights on. *Trust me*, it said, in the day, in the night, in the small and lonely hours, *the world is still here*. Of course he was only a tape, so even if the world were gone his voice might still come on when you dialled 123.

I went downstairs. Amaryllis's puddles were still there. I opened the door, stepped out into the rain, got wet. That didn't prove anything. Was I passing through myself? Had I already done that and come out on the other side? I went back up to the studio. There she was: Lenore at the cliff's edge with the sea behind her. I touched the painting, got paint on my finger.

'Not a glim,' I said. I clapped my hands together, felt myself do it, heard the sound. Had I been sleep-painting? Nothing like this had ever happened before. I looked away from the painting and looked back. Lenore was still there.

Why had Amaryllis run out of the house like that? Evidently she knew Lenore. Did she know about Lenore and me? She'd left the RCA the year before I arrived – that would have been 1992 but she was probably still in touch with people from the school. Life seemed more and more like a Klein bottle.

I picked up the phone again and dialled the number for Rail Enquiries.

29

LOOKING AT SHAPES

Taking a tolerant view of whatever reality was operative at the time and accepting things pretty much at their face value, I found myself the next day on the 13:01 to Flitwick. I was on my way to see Alan Bennett, the Klein-bottle man.

The Thameslink trains left not from the usual King's Cross platforms but from a parallel universe reached by a long corridor from King's Cross tube station and an escalator of doubtful authenticity. Nevertheless, having committed myself to this expedition I persevered, bought a ticket, and was directed to Platform B. This would-be terminus seemed not quite a proper railway station; it was as if someone with a few trains had decided to squat there and had hacked their way into the system to get arrival and departure times posted on legitimate screens.

The Thameslink train turned up right on time carrying more emptiness than passengers. It hurried out of London as if it didn't care where it went; I feared that it might forget Flitwick altogether. Places along the way came and went in a succession of not-herenesses, presenting themselves like a lineup of the usual suspects as the train approached, paused at, then left St Albans, Harpenden, Luton, Leagrave, and Harlington. When a sign said FLITWICK I got off, went up stairs, over a bridge, down stairs and through the life-size model railroad station to the pick-up point where Alan Bennett was waiting in a small red car.

Imagining backwards from the attenuations of Klein-bottlery to their maker I'd arrrived at someone who looked like Basil Rathbone or Peter Cushing. In this I wasn't too far off; Bennett might have been Cushing's younger brother, competent to deal not only with vampires but with strange surfaces as well. He was of middle height, slight in build, had fair hair going grey, and spectacles. His dominant feature was a high domed forehead that looked as if any number of Klein-bottle variations and other topologies might be quietly circulating within. Clearly this kept him in a good humour; he had an easy lightness and brightness about him that made me aware of how heavy and dark I was feeling.

We exchanged the usual arrival remarks as he drove through Flitwick, pointing out pubs and other landmarks and explaining how it had grown, but I wasn't taking in what he said because while he spoke I was thinking, Is life like a Klein bottle? Were Amaryllis and I ever going to be together again to pass through ourselves at the point of intersection? If the bottle is broken, does the passing-through carry on without it?

Bennett's house was in a modern yellow-brick terrace. His wife, Virginia, had the cheerfully unfazable manner of someone who could deal with Klein bottles and Möbius strips without going round the twist. She gave me a cup of tea while their dog, a King Charles spaniel called Amber, having thumped a welcome with her tail, came over to get acquainted. 'Actually,' said Alan when he thanked me for the Glenfiddich I brought, 'I do have a weakness for whisky.'

'I'm glad,' I said, 'because I want to get on the good side of you. I'm hoping you can help me with my Klein-bottle problem.'

'What sort of problem?'

'They trouble me.'

'In what way?'

'I think I might be in one, in a manner of speaking.'

'Looking for a way out?'

'I don't know; I'm confused. Have you ever thought that life is like a Klein bottle?'

'Not that I can remember. Felix Klein described his bottle as "a one-sided surface that is closed and has no boundary". An ant on any part of the surface could walk in any direction without ever going over an edge; there are no edges. Does life seem like that to you?'

I thought of the boundaries and edges in my life; there seemed to be more of them all the time. I grimaced and scratched my head. 'Not really,' I said.

He seemed concerned, rubbed his face a little. 'I doubt that I can help you with your problem, but let's go to my workshop and I'll show you what I do and maybe something will come to you.'

I finished my tea and we stood up. Virginia nodded encouragement. 'Ideas come to Alan at all hours of the day and night,' she said, 'so you never know.' Amber smiled reassuringly and expressed with her tail that everything, if it wasn't already all right, would be all right in the fullness of time. Her life had obviously been different from Queenie's and she was an optimist.

I followed Alan to the workshop which was just outside the house and used to be a garage. I've had people follow me up to my studio the same way, expecting something out of the ordinary, hoping perhaps to see through my eyes something they'd missed with theirs.

As soon as we entered the place I recognised it as one of those magic caves found here and there where enthusiasts of divers kinds devote themselves to alchemy or perpetual motion, the esoterica of clockwork, the images of anamorphism, the observation of celestial bodies or the manufacture of ships in bottles – all manner of disciplines not always listed in the yellow pages.

There were a large lathe and a smaller one and three gas burners whose flames fluttered patiently on standby. Benches and shelves were crowded with tins, bottles, boxes, and various appliances relevant to his work. Several of his non-Kleinian artefacts were on some of the shelves. One of them featured the word CHAOS in glass tubing; when activated by the gravity feed from its little reservoir, blue bubbles went round chaotically inside the glass letters. Nearby stood a small glass fountain patterned on the one invented in antiquity by Hero of Alexandria.

'I guess you've been doing this for a while,' I said.

'I've been in scientific glass-blowing for forty years,' said Alan. 'I left school at fifteen and became an apprentice in a local company, and after a couple of years I was designing or redesigning everything they made. I carried on doing that wherever I worked until I took early retirement in 1995. Since then I've been in business for myself.'

'How did you get started on Klein bottles?'

'Someone showed me one back in my apprentice time and I worked out how to make it – they're not the easiest things to make – and then I didn't think anything more about them until probably 1990. I found out from somewhere that Felix Klein said that if his bottle is cut along the correct line it makes two single-twist Möbius strips. So I thought, If a basic Klein bottle cuts to give two single-twist Möbius strips, what shape would cut to give two three-twist or five-twist? Hence the collection.

'I'd got all the way up to design No. 14 before I realised that if you cut the Klein bottle right across the middle in a straight line you get two Möbius strips – I hadn't recognised that before. The wonderful thing is that if I *had* known where to cut the Klein bottle I'd never have made designs 1 to 14; this is what interests all the mathematicians, because it's a research project done purely in a practical way with no mathematical knowledge at all, simply by looking at shapes, redesigning shapes, and the whole lot's cast in glass and they've got it for ever.'

I tried to think whether I had any for ever in my life. Amaryllis? Doubtful. 'I've stood in front of your display at the Science Museum,' I said, 'and been baffled by it. The sheer intricacy of all those comings and goings in the bottles overwhelmed me.'

'If I show them to you one at a time it'll be easier,' said Alan. He produced one of those black sample cases used by salesmen, started unwrapping the contents, and set down on the nearest free space the basic Klein bottle, the one that I had by now seen from all angles, animated and still, on the various Internet sites where it was featured. It's a nice thing to look at – odd but apparently harmless.

That was No. 1. From there he took me through successive elaborations, each time setting down the example beside the previous one as the glittering array grew in numbers and complexity. As he warmed to his subject his voice took on more and more authority, his eyes grew brighter, and he seemed to grow taller. I watched and listened attentively;

being an idea-and-image man, I always look for the idea in the image and the image in the idea – I don't care which comes first. As he showed me one after the other I tried (and failed) to send my mind through all the turnings. I was intrigued by various of the vessels but it was No. 15 that rang the bell for me.

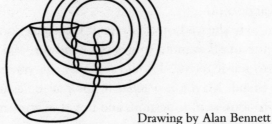

Drawing by Alan Bennett

'This one has five piercings,' he said.

'Passes through itself five times,' I said.

'That's right.'

The vessel he was showing me was shaped like a tumbler, with the mouth at the top becoming a tube that descended through the body of the vessel. It passed through it once, went round to pass through it again, and went round yet again before returning to the main body. That's how it is with Amaryllis and me, I thought: there is the vessel of our two selves; from it they coil outward and return, five times piercing the point of intersection. Those words in my mind seemed to have significance but I wasn't sure what they meant.

'Are any of these helping you with your problem?' said Alan.

'I don't know. What you do is art, and art isn't meant to solve problems, is it.' I didn't really want to talk any more, I wanted to go away and think about No. 15 and

I wanted to be able to look at it while I thought about it.

'Actually,' said Alan after a moment's consideration, 'I wasn't thinking of them as art when I made them. When I made the first fourteen I was just trying to work out where to make the cut for two single-twist Möbius strips. No. 15 happened because it was the next thing to do after No. 14, and so on.'

He showed me the rest of the collection but No. 15 was the one I wanted to get my hands on and I persuaded him to sell it to me. I could feel that this one wanted to be my friend. Maybe it wanted to look at me as much as I wanted to look at it. Questions and hopes of answers had already left my mind; mysteries are the only real satisfaction and this one had agreed to live with me.

Before we left for the station Alan showed me a stone sculpture he'd done that lay in a corner of the garden. It was a compact stubby little man lying on his side with his legs drawn up and one arm shielding his head. It wasn't just a stone figure of a man, it was a little stone man sleeping. Glimming stone glims.

'What do you call it?' I said.

'*The Awakening*,' he replied.

30

SOUVENIR

On the train back to London I put my rucksack in my lap and reached inside it to caress the No. 15 Klein bottle. With my fingers I followed the curving tube of itself as it passed through itself again and again. I was soothed by it; I felt that by touching that hidden mystery I was taking in some secret through my fingers. Yes, I said to myself, this is how it is with the selves of Amaryllis and me.

After a time I fell asleep and found myself on the road through the pine woods approaching the little shack where I'd last seen the old woman posing as a black cat. This time there was a sign over the door: SOUVENIRS.

I opened the door and went in. There was no bell to announce me; the place smelled as if it had been hauled up from the bottom of the sea. From the single window with the blind pulled down came a glaucous dimness in which I made out the old woman, wearing her black poncho and sombrero as always, sitting in a rocker which creaked metronomically.

'I knew you'd be back,' she said. 'Give your old black cat a big kiss.'

'Give me a break,' I said, backing away. Her breath would have knocked over a horse and she needed a shave.

'Horehound drops are good for coughs,' she said. There was a jar of them standing on an old barrel by a small display case in which I saw, behind the smeared glass, a black velvet pillow with script lettering in silver paint:

For you I pine, for you I balsam.

There was nothing else in the place. 'There it is,' she said, 'a souvenir of times gone by. A place to lay your head.' Her voice changed, 'This train is now approaching King's Cross. Please be sure to take all your belongings with you when you leave.'

I began to cry and I was still crying when I woke up. A woman tapped me on the shoulder. Middle-aged, kind face. 'Are you all right?' she said.

'I'm fine,' I said. 'I'm just passing through myself.'

She nodded sympathetically. 'I know it's hard but you can do it, you can take charge of your life. Let me give you this,' and she pressed a copy of *Notes from a Friend* into my hands.

'Thank you,' I said. 'You're a real Samaritan.'

'Always remember,' she said as we left the train, 'the fact that you're alive means that someone cares about you.'

31

A SEAPORT

I hadn't seen or heard from Amaryllis since she'd bolted from my house after seeing Lenore in the painting on my easel. My thoughts were in a turmoil and it was obvious that she'd been greatly disturbed and distressed by the picture. I took it off the easel and leant it against the wall with the back facing out. I was wondering what to do about Amaryllis but so far nothing useful had occurred to me.

I've written about four of the glims I had without her: the Brass Hotel; Venice; the old woman posing as a black cat; and the deserted beach. These were quite strong but mostly the ones I glimmed alone were less interesting. Even in these she often appeared in non-speaking parts, sometimes seen briefly in the distance, sometimes as a picture on the wall or a headline in a newspaper. These were low-budget productions, usually only one or two scenes with a small cast. The major glims, the ones with Amaryllis as the female lead, were vivid, intense, rich in colour and atmosphere, complete in sensory experience, and altogether more real than real.

This was Sunday. Saturday night I had one of my low-budget glims but it was a special one. The colour was very muted and the whole thing was just one quick scene. In it

I had a book of Claude's paintings open at the page with *A Seaport*. My hand held a magnifying glass to the picture and I saw that two of the figures on the strand were Amaryllis and I. The light in the picture changed from late afternoon to dawn and I woke up smiling.

I had no doubt that a visit to the National Gallery would prove auspicious in one way or another. I closed my eyes and saw dim ships in a golden haze so after breakfast I took a Tower Hill train to Embankment and changed there for the Northern Line to Charing Cross. While in the Underground I kept being aware of all the thoughts, all the words and pictures in the heads of other passengers. I didn't want all that buzzing and humming and visual interference but that's the world.

Emerging from Charing Cross station I crossed the road to St Martin-in-the-Fields, rejected the advances of the Brass Rubbing Centre, and nodded to Nelson on his column as I went up the National Gallery steps. I passed through the crowd on the porch, joined the crowd inside, and made my way to Room 15.

On the way I paused at van Hoogstraten's peepshow in Room 17. I check that peephole from time to time and look in on the little dog sitting in the Dutch interior; there are several humans visible through doorways but the dog is the inhabitant who presides over that interior; I like to look through peepholes and I like to be reassured that the little world seen through this one is unchanged. The Dutch painters of the seventeenth century delighted in *trompe-l'oeil*, spatial illusion, and perspective; peep-boxes were done by various masters, and the idea of crooked painting creating the illusion of straight reality is a comfort to me.

In Room 15 there were two Claudes: *Seaport with the Embarkation of Saint Ursula* and *Landscape with the Marriage of Isaac and Rebekah*. The story of Saint Ursula distracted me somewhat from the painting; she was beginning her pilgrimage with eleven ships each carrying one thousand virgins. The women following her were all full-grown and I found myself wondering how large a geographical area would have to be combed to find eleven thousand full-grown virgins, even in an age of faith. The painting was very pleasing but lacked the golden haze I craved. The Isaac and Rebekah marriage seemed under-populated and tame for a Jewish wedding but was full of happy tranquillity. The landscape with its distant mountain and aqueduct, its middle-distant water mill and weir and shining water, and its foreground frame of trees was a delight to the eye, and I suspected that the weir and the water mill symbolised the power of God who makes all the wheels go round and had inspired Rebekah to take a chance on the far-away unknown Isaac and become a camel-order bride.

Still pursuing dim ships and a golden haze, I went on to Room 19 and more Claudes. There I found a half-circle of green-blazered children gathered round a young female teacher in front of *Landscape with Psyche outside the Palace of Cupid*. The children, most of whom looked to be under ten, seemed enthralled as the teacher told them the story of the painting with gestures, facial expressions, and enough italics to sink a battleship. '*Psyche had never seen* her *husband*; he *came* to her *only* in the *hours of darkness* and left *before the dawn* (here some of the children exchanged knowing glances). Her *sisters reminded her* that the *Pythian oracle* had said she *would marry a monster*.'

Breathlessly but never out of breath, the teacher went on to tell her charges how Psyche provided herself with a knife and a lamp, ready to have a look at her sleeping consort before she finished him off. The light revealed the beautiful winged Cupid but a drop of hot oil from the lamp woke him and he spread his wings and flew out of the window. The teacher and Psyche were alike desolated by this and I moved on to the sea and ships. I hadn't thought of the Cupid and Psyche story for a long time, and although I saw myself neither as the one nor the other I was obscurely troubled by it.

Down at the waterfront I saw the Queen of Sheba outward bound in fair weather on a making tide. There also was *A Seaport*, the one with the golden haze: in the westering sunlight of a declining day a ship is moored close to the shore; another rides at anchor in the distance. Farther out stands a tall lighthouse. In the left foreground is a great palazzo with broad curved stairs and a landing stage. Beyond it recede other noble architectures with more ships visible through an arch. The foreground figures on the strand seem theatrical, like an opera chorus before the arrival of the principals. This is one of Claude's all-purpose imaginary seaports, available for conferences, weddings, and the comings and goings of heroes, saints, and royalty. The sketch for this painting, which appears in one of my books, conveys no particular mood, but the atmosphere of the painting is such that it seems at the same time to be waiting for something and saying goodbye to everything. Amaryllis was standing in front of it. The back of her T-shirt said:

The worst never falls short.

I recognised the line from the film *Hommes, femmes, mode d'emploi*. She turned towards me as I approached, and the front of her T-shirt said:

Look thy last on all things lovely,
Every hour . . .

'Fare Well', Walter de la Mare

'Random?' I said.

She looked at me, shook her head, and sighed heavily. 'Support,' she said.

I made a little sound to express that I understood how that was.

'What do you think of this one?' she said, indicating the Claude.

'Well, it seems at the same time to be waiting for something and saying goodbye to everything.'

'Is that how it is with you?'

'Pretty much. You?'

'Pretty much.' Although her eyes were on my face I sensed that she saw over my shoulder Lenore standing at the edge of the cliff. Her own face seemed a reflection in a dark pool; any word of mine might be the stone that would scatter it in broken ripples.

'Actually,' I said, 'I'm waiting for something more than I'm saying goodbye to everything.'

'Every hello has in it a goodbye to the thing before it, wouldn't you say?'

'Yes, I guess I'd say that. Would you have a coffee with me?'

'Today I think I need to feel strange all by myself. I'm going now.'

'OK, see you.'

'Yes,' she said as she walked away. I had coffee in the Brasserie, then went down to the exit where I paused at the

141

Plexiglas-enclosed model of Trafalgar Square, the National Gallery, and their surroundings. ADMISSION IS FREE, said the words bannered across the bottom of the Plexiglas. PLEASE GIVE AS MUCH AS YOU CAN TO HELP US KEEP IT FREE. I called to mind Amaryllis's face and the way she had looked at me just before she left. 'Please,' I whispered, and put a five-pound note into the contribution slot.

I went out into Trafalgar Square, blinking in the sunlight, and was mobbed by pigeons that fluttered and flapped around me like dead thoughts. *Nothing*, shouted the pigeons. *This is all there is, there never was anything else.* One perched on my shoulder, one on my lifted arm. Nearby a van sold PIGEON FOOD, and outbursts of tourists were being St Francis, the women squealing as pigeons landed on them while their husbands, boyfriends, sons, daughters, sisters, brothers, uncles, aunts, cousins, friends and random strangers photographed them with little amateur cameras, larger professional ones, and camcorders. *This is what it's all about*, said the cameras to one another. *SIGHTSEE!* clamoured the passing buses, *THIS IS THE OFFICIAL SIGHTSEEING TOUR! BE SEEN TO BE SIGHTSEEING!*

Boys climbed on to the heads of the bronze lions and slid down their backs, whooping and hollering. Hot-dog vendors offered to the breeze the smell of the one street that is everywhere. Brightly coloured vans supplied SOFT ICE, COLD DRINKS. Small entrepreneurs displayed henna tattoos, hairbands, plastic trolls, jiffy portraits, postcards, prints, and a variety of inexpensive fetish objects. Mallards cruised domestically in the fountains, ignoring the bronze mermaids, mermen, and merchildren. Always the waters jetted into the air, rising and falling to rise and fall again, a little wind from the west blowing the spray on to bystanders at the eastern rim.

Words in many tongues filled the air like locusts but everything in Trafalgar Square was less than the pigeons; they flew, walked, fluttered, hopped, and shat among the St Francises who squealed and hopped and fluttered among them while high above them the ghost of victory still perched on Nelson's shoulder. I felt like a scene in a film where the desperate lover tries to push through a milling crowd as the woman, lost in the throng, disappears for ever. Cleaners in chartreuse hi-vi vests lounged at the edges of the square with their brooms and shovels, uncaring.

She wasn't here. Had I thought she would be? Or had I simply needed to be mobbed by pigeons? I didn't know. She didn't want to be with me at this time, so why was I being the desperate lover in the milling crowd? I was having trouble fitting into the prevailing time and space. Had I perhaps slipped out of reality into something less comfortable? The picture in my eyes seemed to be melting like a film stuck in the projector.

I put my hands over my eyes, took them away. The picture was firm again. A woman was standing in front of me, middle-aged, kind face. Was she the one who'd given me *Notes from a Friend*? Was there a league of them?

'It's real,' she said. 'Even if all of us here close our eyes it won't go away.'

'I read about a tribe somewhere,' I said, 'I think it's in South America: they all glim the same glim.'

'They what?'

'You know, they see the same thing in their sleep.'

'In their dreams?'

'They all have the same one.'

'Every night?'

'I don't know how often they do it. It's their story glim, the story of them. It explains everything.'

'Why do you call it a "glim"?'

'Speech impediment.'

'Maybe it's reality.'

'What?'

'Their dream – maybe reality is a dream and they know how to dream it.'

I closed my eyes again. When I opened them she was gone. It couldn't have been the woman from the train; she wouldn't have said reality was a dream.

32

THE *COMMEDIA DELL'ARTE*

Joni Mitchell used to sing that she didn't know love at all, it was only love's illusions she recalled. So clearly I'm not the only one who's learned that lesson. I suppose if two people share an illusion, then that's their reality for as long as it lasts? It's hard to know where love ends and something else begins; it's also hard to know what's love and what isn't. According to Georg Groddeck, if a man can use the toilet after the woman he loves has just vacated it and not be offended by the smell, that's love. Lenore and I passed that test in the beginning. Smells certainly matter: I remember, when we walked the Troy Town maze that January and I kissed her, the smells of earth after rain, of her cold face, her hair and the black wool scarf she wore. Love-smells.

Lenore was a smoker, not so much when I first knew her but more and more later. When she'd been around the house always smelled smoky and she smelled and tasted of cigarettes but I was willing to overlook it. Things changed as things will but the sex stayed good and there were times when it was our main form of communication. She was a pleasure to look at with her clothes off; she had a wonderful back, long and sinuous, and a callipygian curve that made me forgive her for a lot of things. The nudes I did of her were some of my best; I used to love drawing the snakiness of her and sometimes I called her Lamia which was not her favourite pet name.

Her smoking: she smoked Marlboro Regulars which come in a soft pack rather than a box. When she started a pack she'd pull off the little strip that opened the cellophane, then she'd tear off the bit of silver foil that exposed the first six cigarettes. Some people at that point tap the upside-down pack against the index finger of the other hand to make one of the cigarettes pop up; she didn't: holding the pack right-side-up in her left hand she'd give it a vicious jab in the bottom with her right thumb. I half-expected the Marlboros to cry out and I winced every time she did it.

I've already gone into our conversation about my bird-women. That took place a few months after I asked her to move in with me and she said no. As I think of it now I know we'd have driven each other crazy but at the time her refusal shook me and I had to accept that something had gone out of what we had at the very beginning. People say, 'Let's cut to the chase,' when they want to bypass all the introductory material and get to the heart of the matter but maybe in matters of love the introductory material *is* the heart of the matter – that mutually respectful recognition that doesn't want to lose any of the goodness of the thing by hurrying. Lenore and I had certainly cut to the chase and I know now that something was lost in the process. 'It's how you enter a room that matters,' a woman once said to me, and more and more I think she was right.

Lenore and I had walked the maze and declared it was for ever in January 1993 but by the end of summer what we had between us seemed less and less like love. She rarely showed me her notebooks any more whereas when we were first together she was keen for me to see her notes and sketches almost daily, and even though she tended to be pompous in her remarks about seeing she was almost childishly proud of her sketches and her words and she was eager for my praise. Her drawings were excellent, her verbal observations were sharp, and I was able to say the sort of things she wanted to hear while slipping in a useful comment from time to time.

We did the things that lovers do: we went to concerts and the opera, saw films, drank at pubs, dined at restaurants, cooked for each other, visited museums and the National Gallery, took long walks along the river. Lenore liked Messiaen, Ligeti, Boulez, Birtwhistle ('I have no time,' she asserted, 'for composers who try to please, except when I'm in the mood for Antonio Carlos Jobim'), *Tosca* ('I love it,' she said, 'when she sticks the knife in Scarpia, there's real chemistry there. He was hot to penetrate her but she penetrated him first'), *The Vanishing* ('Women get buried alive all the time in one way or another. He made it happen when he let her out of his sight – he stopped seeing her, stopped *perceiving* her, and that was the beginning of the end for both of them'), the Zetland Arms ('If they have John Smith bitter they ought to have Pocahontas lager'), the Blue Elephant ('I bet in Bangkok they're queuing up at Burger King'), mushroom soup (hers), wiener schnitzel (mine), Tyrannosaurus Rex ('If he'd been able to climb the Empire State Building they might have made a film about him'), Velasquez ('Is her rear view nicer than mine?'), and the Battersea Power Station ('Why don't they stand it right-side-up?').

It's difficult to pinpoint when things began to change; I think it was around the time of our bird-woman conversation. Soon after that Lenore told me she was working on a kind of *commedia dell'arte* series. 'It's in modern dress,' she said, 'the *commedia* one sees every day.' The next time I was at her place she showed me the first painting in the series.

'Pantalone,' she said, 'the silly old man who likes to chase young women.' She'd painted a very sly and shifty-looking me in my usual jeans and polo-neck but sporting the traditional goat's beard and upswept moustache – definitely not the sort of chap you'd want your daughter to be seduced by. The pose was straight out of Callot and I was leering at a girl in very tight jeans who was bending over a portfolio. Mind you, this was in 1994 when I was twenty-eight and Lenore was twenty-two.

'Do you think of me as an old man?' I said.

'Not in years but in style, if you know what I mean: the teacher exercising his *droit du seigneur* with the juiciest girl students.'

'Like you.'

'Yes, like me.'

'As I remember, it was you who made the first move. I can quote your opening gambit verbatim: "Your main attraction," you said to me, "is that you're going to make me unhappy."'

'I was very vulnerable at that time; I'd just broken up with someone I'd been with for two years and I was beginning to see how these things go. Right now it looks as if time has proved me right, doesn't it?'

That one was high and inside and I didn't swing at it. 'Have you done any others in this series?' I said. 'What about Harlequin?'

'Still working on it,' she said, and showed me a canvas in which the figure in the skintight Harlequin costume was remarkably like hers as was the face below the half-mask.

'That's you,' I said, 'and you're not in modern dress.'

'Harlequin is an idea not bound to any particular time. Anyhow, this one is still subject to change.'

That was in August. The school was closed for the summer and we both had more time but we were seeing each other less and less. Lenore kept pretty busy with her *commedia dell'arte* and I was fooling around with ideas for spooky paintings. If you ask somebody to name a spooky painting, nine times out of ten they'll come up with that one by Fuseli with the little short bloke sitting on the woman's chest. There are definitely big openings in that genre and I fancied my chances.

In September, after we were back in the autumn routine, we watched a video one evening at my place, *Hommes, femmes, mode d'emploi*. The central character, Benoît Blanc, is a lawyer, a married man in his forties. A dedicated womaniser, he claims that 'the right woman is many women' and moves from one to the next as soon as he gets bored. Going for an examination for a stomach complaint, he finds himself in the hands of a Dr Nitez who was one of his discards when she was a medical student. There's nothing wrong with him but she switches test results, tells him that he has a tumour, books him into chemotherapy and reduces him from a hearty adulterer to a shadow of himself.

Lenore thought that Benoît Blanc only got what he deserved. 'He was like an Indian collecting scalps,' she said, 'only he was a pussy collector, which is what most men are, really.'

'Including me?'

'Do you think you're so different?'

'Do you think I see you as part of a pussy collection?'

'Maybe not. You're afraid of women, really – your harpy paintings show that. Maybe I'm your tame harpy and I make you feel like a big man because I let you fuck me.'

'You don't sound too happy with me.'

'How perceptive you are.'

'When you said I was going to make you unhappy, was that a self-fulfilling prophecy? Have you made yourself unhappy with me to make it come out right?'

'I said that because I knew it was going to happen.'

'You weren't talking that way when we walked the maze.'

'That was before we'd been together for what is it, nine months?'

'Are you saying that these nine months have been a mistake?'

'God, you're such a lawyer. Talk, talk, talk. I need a rest from your constant chatter, I need some breathing space.'

'That's a good idea: I think you should go somewhere and breathe for a good long time, maybe ten years or so, then maybe you'll feel a little better.'

'Are you saying this is it for us?'

'Well, I don't see anybody else in this room, do you?'

'Right.' She turned her back on me, slid her knickers down, and flipped up her skirt. 'Take a good look,' she said. 'That's the last you'll see of it.'

'That looks like the end, all right,' I said.

And she was gone. The next day she drove to Beachy Head and jumped off.

33

WHEN I REMEMBER

When I remember Lenore I guess it's love's illusion I recall but I'm baffled by it. How could I commit myself for ever in January and be glad to end it in September? Well of course it was Lenore who brought the for ever into it when we walked the maze. A wiser man would have struck that clause out of the contract; had I been thinking with something other than my brain?

No, that's the usual simplistic answer. My problem was that I always needed to be in love, in the first flush of it, the qualifying heat of it. When that wore off I was ready to move on. I haven't mentioned here the women before Lenore: Amanda; Sophie; Gillian; Catherine; Delphine; Sarah and others going back to the very mists of puberty. The fact is that by 1994 I still hadn't achieved grown-upness.

And there's still more to be said: if I had behaved differently I don't think she'd have killed herself. Yes, she seemed to get some perverse satisfaction out of unhappiness and she was certainly a difficult person to be with but if she had done her usual numbers with a better man she might still be alive. Sometimes between two people it's as if one is a lock and one is a key and they take turns being lock and key; but at other times it's as if both are keys or both are locks and nothing can be done. Still, I think *something* could have been done if I'd been a better man, if my love had been more giving and less taking. She needn't have killed herself, and I blamed myself for her death.

34

ABSENT FRIENDS

From the National Gallery and Trafalgar Square I went, for no particular reason, to the Zetland Arms and Amaryllis was there; it was that kind of a day. When she saw me she smiled, flung her hands up in a gesture of resignation, and motioned to me to join her.

'Sorry about this,' I said. 'I didn't come here looking for you.'

'Even if you did it's all right – if this is how it is, this is how it is.'

'In a way it's like Klein bottle No. 15.'

'Which one is that?'

I took it out of my rucksack and held it out to her. 'Take it in your hands,' I said. By now it had become a fetish object for me; when I held it I seemed to feel in it a mystical connection between Amaryllis and me.

'I'd rather not,' she said, not looking me in the eye. With colour, with lights and smoke and shadows, with music and voices, the Zetland Arms enmazed our thoughts and silences as we moved towards and away from the centre, circling between the whisky yew and the bitter holly.

'What are you afraid of?' I said.

'Everything.' She was looking into the distance while sliding her thumb and middle finger up and down her glass.

'Why won't you look me in the eye?'

'Because I'm afraid of everything. I wish Queenie were here.'

'Why?'

'She helped me believe in the world.'

A young man at the next table, wearing a blue-striped shirt with a white collar and an upwardly mobile tie, leant towards us and said, 'Forgive me for eavesdropping, but were you talking about the old bull-terrier bitch that used to come in here with Fred Scoggins?'

'Probably,' I said.

'Both of them are no longer with us; she died and Scoggins put a rope round his neck and kicked the chair away.'

Amaryllis was crying.

'Sorry,' said our informant. 'Were you friends of his?'

'Yes,' I said, 'we were. Thank you for that graphic report.'

'Sorry,' he said again. 'I'll leave you to yourselves,' and he withdrew to a distant table.

Amaryllis found a wadded-up handkerchief in her shoulder bag, blew her nose. 'We weren't really friends,' she said.

'Compared to that bloke we were. You know, it's possible to get along quite well without believing in the world, so long as you're careful crossing the road and so on.'

'Great,' she said. 'Thank you so much, that solves all my problems. Listening to you talk bollocks is a great comfort to me.'

'Speaking of problems,' I said, 'even though the Pines Motel didn't rate too many stars, things seemed pretty good between us when you turned up at my place in the rain. Then you looked at that painting and threw up and off you went.'

154

'Stomach thing,' she said. 'I really wasn't feeling too well, and suddenly all the studio smells got to me.'

'Smells can do that, I know.'

'I was expecting to see a painting of me on the easel. What happened to it?'

'Let me get a refill for you and a drink for me and I'll tell you about it.'

Life gets tricky when you have to think too much about what you're going to say, and I was grateful for a few minutes' respite as I watched the barman draw the pints.

When I got back to the table I raised my glass. 'Here's looking at you?' I said with a question mark.

'Absent friends,' she replied. We clinked glasses and glances. 'The painting?' she said.

'It's very strange – the painting of you seems to have changed into the one you saw on the easel.'

'Seems to have changed?'

'Well, it was certainly painted by me, but I've no idea how it happened. I wasn't drunk or stoned but I must have got into some kind of altered state.'

She looked at that explanation a little askance but let it pass. 'Did you know Lenore well?'

'Pretty well. You?'

'Pretty well. I don't suppose anyone knew her well enough to be able to give her what she needed.'

'Any idea what that might have been?'

Amaryllis shook her head. We looked at each other, looked away, drank our drinks, sidled away from the subject of Lenore.

Amaryllis looked at her watch. 'I'm going to the Little Angel Theatre to see *The Sleeping Beauty*,' she said. 'I've booked two seats just in case. Want to come?'

'Sure. Sounds like our kind of show.'

'I've always wondered about the story, wondered about her dreams through all those years when she was asleep. Did she dream she was awake? Even the flies in the castle were asleep, and the great tall hedge growing all around and shutting it off from the world. I never got to see a play of it when I was a child and I feel like seeing one now.'

So we finished our drinks and went to South Ken for the Piccadilly Line. The train rumbled and mumbled to itself, and at Knightsbridge a thin girl with long dark hair and an accordion got on. She was wearing jeans and a T-shirt that said, *Oh Galuppi, Baldassaro* . . .

'What do you reckon?' I asked Amaryllis.

'I think she's waiting for a suitable person to turn up and complete the quotation. What do you think she's going to play?'

'She looks like a Scarlatti type, maybe Soler.'

The carriage wasn't crowded; the girl took up a position between the central doors with plenty of space around her. She opened the accordion first, then her mouth, and sang '*Plaisirs d'amour*' while she accompanied herself. Her voice, vinegary-sweet, made lamplight and shadows. Everybody stopped talking and listened. We looked in vain for someone to come round to collect money but there was no one. She finished the song, reprised it with the accordion alone, closed the instrument, smiled, and got off at Hyde Park Corner.

35

THE WOOD-DAEMON

The Little Angel Theatre seats a hundred and it was pretty full. The audience were middle-class children with a handful of adults who had apparently herded them there on the car-pool principle. The stage was in plain view before the performance; on it the king and queen sat in the main room of the castle. To the left was the tower, its three-storey interior exposed like that of a doll's house.

The puppeteers appeared and were applauded as they took their places on the bridge. The backcloth they stood behind was only waist-high, so their hands and faces were clearly visible throughout the performance. A woman sat at a spinet to provide the music.

As the house lights dimmed and the play began Amaryllis immediately identified with the marionettes. 'Hands above them work the strings,' she whispered. 'Mouths above them speak their words. What an awful way to live.'

'They're not alive, Amaryllis,' I whispered back, 'they're marionettes made of wood.'

'I know that, but they *are* the story; the story lives in them. And between shows they hang on hooks in the darkness without movement, without voices. How would *you* like that?'

'Not much,' I said, and we settled back to follow the action. The story went its slow way; the audience were attentive and responsive; they laughed as a frog joined the queen in her bath and promised that after many childless years she would at last have one. When the princess was born the wise women were invited to the celebration but one was turned away because the royal household was one silver plate short.

The wise women who were welcomed were all rather ineffectual little things in gauzy pastel frocks but the odd one out was three times as big as they, wore vivid red and purple, had three twisty horns growing out of her head, and was clearly someone to be taken seriously.

On being denied a place at the table the three-horned wise woman was very cross indeed and said that the princess on her fifteenth birthday would prick her finger with a spindle and die. The other wise women managed to plea-bargain that down to one hundred years of sleep for the princess and everybody in the castle, even the flies.

When the prince came looking for her after a succession of losers he encountered a wood-daemon, a green satyr who tried to confuse him. First the wood-daemon claimed to be the princess, then he said the prince was dreaming. 'I'm awake!' said the prince. 'No,' said the wood-daemon, 'you're asleep and you're dreaming that you're awake.' The wood-daemon, though ostensibly sylvan, was quite urbane, and it was plain to see that he enjoyed his verbal joust with the prince. His red eyes glowed; he had horns and goat-legs and a long tail; he seemed to have an inner darkness that was not child's play; altogether he seemed more of a personage than the other marionettes.

Not to be deterred, the prince pressed on, found the hedge which opened for him, and made his way to the tower bedroom of the princess. When he kissed her she woke up and said, 'I dreamed that I was a princess.'

'You dreamed what you are,' said the prince, and shortly after that they were married, the house lights came up, and the children were taken to their various homes by their parents or those *in loco parentis*.

'I keep seeing those hands dancing in the shadows above them,' said Amaryllis afterwards. 'And the faces above the hands – you could see their mouths moving when the marionettes spoke.'

'You'll feel better when you have something to drink,' I said, and we cut through St Mary's churchyard, crossed the road and went into the King's Head. This pub, which houses a theatre, sports spotlights as well as the usual sort of lamps but the spots aren't too bright, the pale-brown woodwork is polished, mellow, neatly joined and takes the light nicely, and the effect is intimate. There was no music, just a low murmur of conversation. Through the windows the Islington Sunday afternoon could be seen going its quiet way.

'The glims she must have had in those hundred years of sleep!' said Amaryllis as we sat down at a table.

'She glimmed what she was,' I said.

'Glimmed she was asleep and glimming?' said Amaryllis.

'Woodenly,' I said, and went to the bar for our drinks.

'The wood-daemon was the one I liked the best,' said Amaryllis when I returned. 'The others were just wooden actors, but you could see that when he was carved the wood-daemon spirit entered him and he became it. His red eyes glowed and his face had in it the wood-darkness and the wood-fear even when he was fooling around with the prince. The world *is* a dark wood that we're lost in, don't you think?'

I leant over and kissed her.

'What was that for?' she said.

'We'll hold hands through the dark wood, Amaryllis,' I said, 'and maybe we'll find our way out. Or we'll build a little hut and live there in the heart of the wood.'

'There *was* a hut in the wood by the dark road we glimmed; in real life there was – a little shack that sold souvenirs and we stopped there that time on holiday when I was little. It was a time when everything was cosy, everything was nice. They bought me horehound drops and a black-velvet pillow with silver script lettering on it: *For you I pine, for you I balsam.*' She pronounced balsam the American way: *bawl some*. 'I loved that pillow, the way it smelled as I fell asleep.'

'Where is it now?'

'Gone. The good time went and that went with it.' As she told me this her face became what it must have been when she was twelve or thirteen. 'Ah!' I said involuntarily, and looked around to see if anyone else had noticed. They hadn't.

'What?' said Amaryllis.

'Nothing. How did the good time go?'

'My dad walked out, and nothing was the way it used to be. Sometimes I saw him in glims, just ordinary ones, and he would hug me and start to tell me something but I'd always wake up before he said it. Then this new thing happened to me; I've told you about when I was thirteen and I pulled my English teacher. I was just a scrawny little thing back then and boys had never paid much attention to me but they did when I started pulling them and doing what I'd done with the English teacher, only more. They all got interested in me then; they didn't know I was pulling them, they thought they were having those glims because there was something about me that got them excited. Some of the bolder ones tried their luck with me after school in the unglim and I made their wildest glims come true. Pretty soon I had all the boys I wanted and the other girls were going crazy trying to figure it out. That's not very Pre-Raphaelite, is it?'

'Amaryllis, why are you telling me all this?'

'Maybe I want to see if I can make you fall out of love with me.'

'Why would you want me to fall out of love with you?'

'Because being in love is something anybody can do hundreds of times. I've fallen in love and out of love over and over and it came to nothing. So now I want to find out what comes to something. I'm empty.'

I went to the bar for whiskies and pints of bitter and salt-and-vinegar crisps. While I was waiting for the pints I listened to two men next to me. 'They wanted to know how old I was,' said one of them. 'I told them I played late thirties which was what the part called for. They said they'd let me know and they gave me that look that means the phone will never ring.'

'I'm thinking of opening a restaurant,' said the other, 'if I can find a couple of backers.' Over the road St Mary's Church was standing up under its whipped-cream steeple; the buses were running; Islington was doing its Sunday-afternoon thing and I appreciated that: if everything would do its thing at the proper time the world would be a safer place.

When I got back to the table Amaryllis downed her whisky as if it were lemonade, took a long snort of bitter, and continued. 'My mother got married again. There was a man who wrote a book called *The Sixty-four Dramatic Plots*; I don't know if he included the one with the mother, the teenage daughter, and the stepfather with the hots for the daughter.'

'Nabokov did that one.'

'His name was Nigel and he used to pick his nose and eat it. Everybody draws the line somewhere. I cleared out and I haven't seen my mother since. I haven't simply been whoring around but I keep needing to be in love and maybe that's the same thing. Now I haven't told you everything but I've told you more than I've ever told anyone else.'

'Maybe we could stop talking about love,' I said, 'and just think of being with each other.'

She reached for my hand and squeezed it. 'From here on out, you said once.'

'I'm still saying it.'

'I'm thinking about the shop where I got the pillow. I still remember the smell of it.'

'Why'd you leave it behind?'

'I was leaving my childhood behind and that was part of it.'

'And you want to go back to that souvenir shop where you first saw it because you felt good there.'

'Yes, but you don't want to go there, do you.'

'No, I don't.'

'Is it a place you've been to?'

'Yes, or one like it, but it would have been a long time before you were there. Who was behind the counter in that shop?'

'A girl of eighteen or so. There was an old woman all in black in a rocking chair with a kitten in her lap.'

'A black kitten?'

'Yes. Do you think it was the same place?'

'Could have been.'

'Why don't you want to go there?'

I told her and she looked thoughtful. 'I can understand how you feel,' she said.

'In my mind the ride in the car, the red sunset and the woman singing on the radio and the old woman in the souvenir shop, the black cat and the pillow are all part of the deaths of my father and mother.'

She nodded.

'On the other hand,' I said, 'I'd like to keep you company if you want to go there. Let me think about it for a bit.'

We left the King's Head and walked down Upper Street to the Angel. On the way we paused at Islington Green and the statue of Sir Hugh Myddelton. 'Have you ever noticed,' said Amaryllis, 'that whenever you see a statue of a man in doublet and hose, he's got really good legs? But men's legs aren't always that good, I've seen lots that would look terrible in doublet and hose. I wonder if the sculptors sometimes made them look a bit better than they were.'

'I'm sure of it,' I said. 'You can't trust artists.'

At the Angel it takes two escalators to get down to the Northern Line platforms. The first one may well be the longest in London. Amaryllis stood in front of me as we escalated down and I looked over her head at the longitudinal lines on the pale-green arched ceiling and the fluorescent panels on each side all dwindling to a vanishing point somewhere below the floor at the bottom. I was remembering the vanishing points on the night roads I'd travelled with Lenore. Perspective being what it is, there are vanishing points wherever you look, it's just that you don't notice them so much unless you see parallel lines apparently converging in the distance. Lines from a Shriekback song came to mind: '*One day soon you and I will merge – everything that rises must converge.*'

We went up to King's Cross and changed to the Piccadilly Line for Earl's Court where we got a Wimbledon train to

Fulham Broadway and home. Travelling in three different trains with escalators in between, we were very quiet, holding hands and moving comfortably in a little house of unspoken, a cosy place that we hadn't been to before.

When we got home I could feel that Amaryllis was glad to be there. Until now in the unglim there had always been a varying hedge around her castle, sometimes high and sometimes low but always there. Now there seemed to be none, and I got us drinks as soon as possible to keep it that way.

'Here's how,' I said, raising my glass.

'Here's how what?' said Amaryllis.

'I don't know, it's just something people say or used to say where I come from. Maybe it just means here's how we do it.'

'Do what?'

'Drink a drink, I suppose.'

'Is that all?'

'What else did you have in mind?'

'Mmmmhmmhmm,' she said. 'Here's how,' and we clinked glasses. She took her shoes off and sat on the couch with her feet tucked under her. As she made herself comfortable she was stretching and squirming languorously and looking at me in a way I'd seen before only in glims.

I know I've mentioned the paintings of John William Waterhouse often enough before this but I don't think I've done him justice in the matter of the depth and individuality of his women: they're all beautiful but not uniformly so; sweetness they all have but darkness as well and a powerful sexuality; any one of them could lead a man to somewhere he'd never get back from.

'I'm feeling a bit more like my glim self today,' said

Amaryllis. I took her naked feet in my hands and something like electricity surged through me.

'Do you remember what I said on the dark road?' she said.

'Please refresh my memory,' I said, kissing her feet.

'Everything north and south of my tattoo is yours,' she murmured. (Have I said how enchanting her murmur was?) 'Also east and west. Front and back included. Do you know why?'

'Tell me.'

'Because I love you.'

She said that! She said it in the unglim! I felt as the Wright brothers must have felt at Kitty Hawk when their frail machine for the first time took the air and, however briefly, left the earth behind.

36

MUSICAL INTERLUDE

The *allegretto* from Beethoven's Seventh might answer here.

37

IT HAPPENS

'It happens,' said Amaryllis. 'Don't worry about it.'

'You can say that,' I said. 'You can be gracious and I appreciate it but you can't feel how I feel. You're the woman I love, the most beautiful woman I've ever known; I've lusted after you since I first saw you in a glim; I've made love to you in glims; now here you are in real life and I couldn't rise to the occasion.'

She took my face in her hands and kissed me. 'In a way it's a kind of compliment – making love to me was so important to you that you were overwhelmed by it. But what didn't happen this time will happen another time, so stop fretting and just be comfortable with me now.'

Not for the first time I felt that I was the boy and she was the teacher. She held my head to her breast and cuddled me and all my cares seemed to slide away. 'Does that feel good?' she said.

'It feels lovely, Amaryllis.'

'Just let me hold you like this for a while. Shall I tell you a story?'

'Yes, tell me a story.'

'This is one that always makes me laugh; it's from your country. Have you read Uncle Remus?'

'Yes, I have. Which story are you going to tell me?'

'This is the one about Brer Fox and Brer Rabbit and the Tar-Baby. Do you like that one?'

'It's one of my favourites. I'm surprised that you know it.'

'It was read to me by a friend who owns the book.'

'An English friend?'

'Yes. Shall I begin?'

'Do,' I said. With my face against her breast I felt the vibrations of her voice as she spoke.

'Well,' she said, 'as you must remember, Brer Rabbit had been outwitting Brer Fox in all kinds of ways for a long time. But Brer Fox had quite a good idea for getting the better of Brer Rabbit.' Here she slipped into the dialect as she continued. '*Brer Fox, he got 'im some tar, en mix it wid some turkentime, en fix up a contrapshun wat he call a Tar-Baby . . .*' She did the whole story faultlessly, right up to Brer Rabbit's triumphant '*Bred en bawn in a brier-patch, Brer Fox — bred en bawn in a brier-patch!*' pronouncing the words exactly as I did the last time I read it aloud.

'Wonderful,' I said. 'Where did you learn that pronunciation?'

'I did it the way it was read to me. Are you sleepy?'

'I am a bit.'

'Maybe we could have a little kip and you could glim us a bit farther down that dark road past the Pines Motel.'

'To the souvenir shop, Amaryllis?'

'Peter . . .' she said.

'What?'

'The bad places in the past, if you don't go to them, do you think they come to you?'

'Probably. Has that happened to you?'

'Not yet but I'm afraid it's going to.'

'A very bad place?'

'Very bad. That's why I want to glim back to that souvenir shop where I felt so good, where everything was cosy.'

'To build up your resistance?'

'It would make me stronger, I know that. The places in childhood where everything is nice, they're like strong magic. Is the souvenir shop a dangerous place for you or is it just depressing?'

'No more than that – it isn't dangerous. If glimming there will make you stronger let's do it.'

She hugged me. 'You're a real comrade, Peter. I've never had one before.'

I kissed her. 'You do now, Amaryllis. Shall we?'

'First,' she said, 'have you got a pen and a bit of paper?'

I gave them to her.

'My name is Amaryllis Fyfe,' she said as she wrote. 'This is my address in Beaufort Street. This is my phone number. This time we can sleep in the same bed when we do it.'

'Do you want to start the glim or shall I?'

'I feel better when you do it.'

When we were in bed I had nothing in mind except glimming but somehow having her name and address and telephone number put new spirit into me. One thing led to another, love made the leap from glim to reality and it was some time before we fell asleep.

38

FINSEY-OBAY

We were on that dark road again. The Pines Motel was somewhere behind us, the souvenir shop somewhere ahead. The air seemed to quiver, the breeze on my face was cool; I breathed deeply, filling my lungs with the freshness of the pines. There was a full moon, white and serene like a goddess, wreathed in pearly clouds.

'The globe of night is all around us,' said Amaryllis, 'and we're inside it with all the colours of darkness. Maybe the wood-daemon is keeping pace with us through the pines.' Her voice had taken on a timbre of the night. The hooting of an owl, the chirping of crickets, were sounds that I could almost taste. The feel of the road under my feet was like the beating of drums.

Amaryllis took my arm, put it round her waist, and pressed close to me. 'Our first time in real life,' she said, 'was it as good as our glims?'

'Reality with you is better than my wildest glims,' I said, and kissed her.

'I'm a very unsure person, Peter. What we have, is it different from what you've had with others?'

'Yes, it's different in all kinds of ways – you're not like

anyone I've ever known and I'm not the same as I was before I met you.'

'How are you different?'

I needed a few moments to find the right word. 'I'm more edgewise than I used to be.'

'I've always been edgewise and slanty but I've been other things too. I hope I'm a different Amaryllis now.'

Hearing our words I felt nervous – they seemed the sort of things people say just before their plane crashes into a mountain. I grabbed her and we hugged and kissed some more. Then I held her at arm's length to read her T-shirt. It said:

We gave three heavy-hearted cheers, and blindly plunged like fate into the lone Atlantic.
Herman Melville, *Moby Dick*

'What does it say?' she asked.

I told her.

'Have you got a drawer labelled Doubts and Misgivings?' she said with her eyes on my face.

'You're not the only unsure person in this outfit, Amaryllis.'

'Are you scared?'

'Yes, I am.'

'Of what?'

'Losing you.'

'How do you think you could lose me?'

'I don't know; I think I'm afraid of losing you because not losing you is the most important thing in the world to me.'

'I'm not sure I'd be that much of a loss, Peter.'

'You don't know what you are to me, Amaryllis.'

'What am I to you?'

I could see a light in the distance, yellow and pink and orange, like a Japanese lantern. I hadn't meant to glim it and I tried to will it away but it kept coming. 'Amaryllis,' I said, 'I know that you don't think much of yourself; I don't think much of myself either. But if the two of us, imperfect as we are, can be true to each other . . .'

She made a sound as if the breath had been knocked out of her. 'Peter,' she said, 'you know that I love you, but if this is truth time I have to say that the one thing I've never been is true to anyone.'

'Neither have I, but if this whole thing is different maybe that can change too.'

Amaryllis clung to me and murmured, 'Do you remember, Peter, at the Brass Hotel that time, how you said we were together from here on out to wherever?'

'I remember.'

'Where do you think wherever will be?'

'Forget wherever, Amaryllis – we're together from here on out, no end to it,' I said as the Finsey-Obay bus loomed over us, 'but I don't think we'll get to the souvenir shop tonight.'

When she saw the bus Amaryllis's face twisted with anger and disbelief, I'd never seen that look before. 'This is your glim, Peter; you were meant to be looking after me. Now you've finished us off.'

'I didn't set out to make this happen,' I said, 'but surely it's not the end of the world – the last time we took this bus we had quite a pleasant evening at the Brass Hotel.'

'You don't understand: this is something else altogether – this is the big one; this time we didn't wait at the bus stop, it came looking for me and your glim wasn't strong enough

to stop it.' She shook her head and sighed. 'Never mind, it's
not your fault – sooner or later it would have come for me
wherever I was.'

'It's me that it's come for,' I said. I tried to pull Amaryllis
away from the bus but we were already inside and she was
climbing the stairs. I looked back towards the doorway but
there was no doorway. 'It's only paper,' I said, and kicked it
as hard as I could. The paper gave like rubber but didn't tear.
'This is my glim,' I said, 'and I can't do anything with it.'

Amaryllis paused and looked down at me. 'It isn't your
glim any more,' she said. 'This is something that was in both
of us, waiting to happen. When you put us on this road you
turned it loose and now it's out, all because I wanted to visit
that wretched souvenir shop.'

We climbed until the stairs came to an end. There were
seats, all of them empty. There were no windows in the paper
sides of the bus, no way to see where we were. We sat down
and felt the glim close in around us. The candle flames shook
in the bamboo chandelier and the shadows jumped with the
rocking of the bus as it gathered speed.

'Weren't there windows last time?'

'No. Anyhow it doesn't matter; we both know where this
bus is going, don't we, Peter?'

'Finsey-Obay.'

'We might as well call it by its right name: Beachy Head,
where Lenore stepped off the edge. I didn't know you were
the one before me until I saw that painting.'

'And I didn't know you were her next one until you told
me the Tar-Baby story.'

'Why did you say you were the one this bus had come
for, Peter?'

'Because I killed Lenore.'

'No, you didn't.'

'Yes, I did. The last time she came to my place we were on the edge of a cliff but I was too stupid to see it; I pushed her over as surely as if I'd gone to Beachy Head with her and done it with my two hands. Now this bus is going to the edge she jumped from and you shouldn't be on it.'

'Yes, I should. It wasn't you, Peter – I'm the one who killed Lenore. When I tried to end it with her she wouldn't let go: she was always ringing me up and she'd come round and make terrible scenes. One night I glimmed the two of us at Beachy Head – I hadn't meant to pull her. There was a full moon shining on the sea and a cold wind blowing. Lenore was standing at the edge of the cliff and shivering. She said, "Happiness never worked for me and neither does unhappiness," then suddenly there was empty space where she'd been. The next morning in the unglim she was found dead at the base of the cliffs.'

'Amaryllis,' I said, 'you can't be sure you made it happen – your glim could have been clairvoyance.'

'But it wasn't, and that wasn't the first time I killed someone. Months after I'd left home I pulled my stepfather into a glim and stabbed him with a kitchen knife and in the morning he was dead from a heart attack. And before Lenore there were two others who died. Ron Hastings and Cindy Ackerman are alive because they didn't try to hold on to me. So you see, Peter, I really am a deadly nightshade.'

'All right, so I'm in love with a deadly nightshade. I don't care what you've done, Amaryllis, and I don't feel like going to Finsey-Obay just now so I'm going to say the d-word – I'm going to STOP THIS DREAM.'

Nothing changed. The candle flames fluttered and the paper walls rippled in the wind as the bus sped towards the end of its route. Amaryllis touched my face. 'I've told you, this glim belongs only to itself now, and we haven't much time. I'm no good, Peter – I've always needed to be in love and I've always fallen out of love before the other person was ready for it to end. I've gone from this one to that one, men and women both, whoever was available until I found you. Think what might happen if I fell out of love with you: I'd never consciously harm you but who knows what I might glim?'

I reflected on that, then I heard myself say, 'If you fall out of love with me I don't care what happens.' I was surprised to hear that but I meant it.

'I don't know how to believe in permanence, Peter,' she said softly, but I thought her words lacked conviction. She turned a little away from me, put her hand over her eyes, and withdrew into her thoughts.

The candle flames fluttered, the paper walls of the bus rippled in the wind, the silence rushed forward with us. What a ridiculous thing, I thought – to die in a glim! This bus would take us over the edge at Beachy Head and on Monday morning Mrs Quinn would find us dead and no one would know what had happened.

Think, I said to myself. If this glim has come out of both of us then the parameters of what's possible and what isn't are in our two minds. She's thinking of what she's going to do. What am I going to do? The motion of the bus was changing, twisting as it went.

'We're close to the edge now, Peter,' said Amaryllis, 'we're passing through ourselves.'

I couldn't speak. My stomach churned and all the nights and days, all the faces and voices, all the names and words, all the promises and lies of past loves surged up out of me in a vomiting that I couldn't stop. My past heaved up and wracked me with the pains of regret, the pangs of shame. What had it all been about, this that would no longer stay down? What had I given, what taken? Had anyone been better off for knowing me?

The same thing was happening to Amaryllis, she too was open-mouthed and helpless, spewing out her self in a torrent of words and weeping as the bus shook and swayed towards the end of its journey. 'Amaryllis!' I gasped.

'What?'

'If we could . . .'

'If we could what, Peter?'

'If we could make it all be different . . .'

'No, Peter.' She was calm now, her face was so loving, so bright! 'It's too late for me but not for you.' She turned and ran back down the stairs with me following. When she could reach the chandelier she grabbed a candle and thrust it into the paper wall. The paper burst into orange, pink, and yellow flames as she planted a foot in my back and shoved me through the fire. 'Goodbye, Peter,' she said, but I grabbed her ankle and pulled her with me and we fell to the ground at the edge of the cliff as the burning bus went over. The flames were pale in the dawn as the sun came up over the grey and shining sea and we woke up on the floor in a tangle of bedclothes.

Amaryllis is one of those women who look good in the morning. On this particular morning she was more beautiful than anything I'd ever seen. 'Be honest with me,' she said. 'Are we dead?'

'I don't think so. What would you like for breakfast?'

'Boilermakers?' she said shyly. What a woman.

A NOTE ON THE AUTHOR

Russell Hoban is the author of many extraordinary novels including *Turtle Diary*, *Riddley Walker*, and most recently, *Angelica's Grotto*. He has also written some classic books for children including *The Mouse and his Child* and the Frances books. He lives in London.

A NOTE ON THE TYPE

The text of this book is set in Bembo. This type was first used in 1495 by the Venetian printer Aldus Manutius for Cardinal Bembo's *De Aetna*, and was cut for Manutius by Frances Griffo. It was one of the types used by Claude Garamond (1480-1561) as a model for his Romain de L'Université, and so it was the forerunner of what became the standard European type for the following two centuries. Its modern form follows the original types and was designed for Monotype in 1929.